1

For information, address Venture Galleries, LLC, 1220 Chateau Lane, Hideaway, TX.

ISBN   978-1-937569-35-8

FCEtier

J. C. Etier (signature)

The
Tourist
Killer

Tammy,
    I hope you enjoy
meeting Claudia.
    Remember —
Be careful where you
go on vacation.

3

Chip

4

The Louisville Tavern is now closed.

Dedication:
To my wife, Miss Bob Etier. She is my soul and my heart's inspiration.

Acknowledgements:
Miss Bob Etier, Buffy Reilly, John Rotan, Roger Hicks, David Swentzel, Bryan Ellis, Kate Kennon, Dr. Wayne Rowe, Doug Carter, Robert Tilford, Ed Hamilton, Art Hoffman

Special notes of thanks:
To Lee Leasure for the inspiration of a ninja.
To Caleb Pirtle III for encouraging me to write and then motivating me to finish my first novel.
To David Ammons for original art work.
To Blue Ridge Books of Waynesville, NC for the use of their reading room.

PROLOGUE

The shooter watched from a distance and thought over the background information obtained through months of surveillance and intense research. If the target stuck to her pattern, the two women would leave the club and go straight to the apartment. It was rare for serial killers to stray from their established patterns.

A gentle summer breeze ruffled the decorative flags outside the buildings along Patton Avenue in Asheville. It brushed the faces of pedestrians along Grove Street as they walked along without fear in the late evening. By nine-thirty, it was dark — even with daylight savings time. Revelers still celebrating the Fourth of July enjoyed the safe environment of the late night downtown area.

So it was for the shooter, too. It had taken at least six months to compile a complete dossier on Sarah Archer, referred to by four different newspapers as "The Slasher."

Six states.
Nine women.
Five years.

She looked little different from most women who walked the streets, attractive enough for men to notice, not pretty enough for them to remember.

Five foot nine.
Muscular.
Agile.
Short, narrow nose.
Dimple on her chin.
Smooth skin.
No make-up.

Tonight, the shooter noted when Sarah Archer walked into the downtown bar, she had accentuated her eyebrows and lashes.

The target may have looked feminine.

She wasn't.

She had been known to overpower victims much larger than she. Sarah, if the police reports were accurate, would get

13

them intoxicated either with drugs or alcohol before making her move.

In every known previous case, she had rented an apartment and lured her target there.

The shooter had been on her trail since February. It was July now. It was unusual to have to do so much legwork. Most of the assignments were more straightforward. The fee for this job would be well-earned. It was now eleven thirty-seven. From her secluded perch atop the Downtown Inn on Patton street, the shooter had a clear view and a variety of shooting angles. The custom-made suppressor would mute most of the report. If the shot was made from the rooftop, most would think it just another firecracker, or maybe another car backfiring in the night.

When alone, the shooter often spoke out loud, not much more than a whisper, but spoken aloud. It provided an affirmation. It helped with her concentration.

Almost midnight — aha. There they go.

Tonight, the shooter saw through the scope, Sarah was a platinum blonde. She wore a tight-fitting mini-skirt and a white, collared blouse.

Pick-up attire.

Through the scope, the shooter could see that Sarah had unfastened several buttons, revealing perhaps a bit too much of her smallish breasts. As the two women exited Scandals, one of Western Carolina's more popular gay/lesbian clubs, they walked hand-in-hand down Grove Street.

It was a clear shot.

Squeeze the trigger.

Then vanish.

The shooter had become a master of escape.

Sarah's companion staggered for a moment — into the line of fire.

Damn.

Sarah helped her date regain her balance and they continued down the street.

Right towards the Slasher's apartment. I'll get her on the sidewalk. The shooter adjusted the rifle to reacquire the target

14

now moving towards Patton Avenue.

Sarah's new friend was an inch or two taller and a few pounds heavier. She, too, was dressed in what the shooter referred to as *pick up attire.*

Gail Oppenheimer was wearing cut-off jeans and a ragged guinea tee. Her coal black hair cascaded down her back and around her shoulders.

She looks a lot more feminine than Sarah does. The shooter waited. Patience had become an art. *Now, I've got her.*

But as the shooter's finger tightened against the trigger, Sarah leaned in close to Gail's ear and whispered. A dark Buick eased up beside them and stopped at the light.

Gail giggled. The shooter relaxed.

Another missed opportunity.

The clock was ticking.

The shooter immediately hurried to the edge of the roof, slipped through an attic window, and ran down two flights of stairs, heading for hotel room three-twenty-six. It had to be a hasty and efficient relocation. No time to spare. The room had a great view — of Sarah's apartment building. The shooter had made sure of it.

The shooter glanced out the window. Now the women were at the street level door. The shooter knelt and waited for the right time to fire. It wouldn't be long now.

As the couple approached the sidewalk entrance, the doorman stepped into the cross hairs.

Damn.

The women swept through the big front glass doors and disappeared into the hotel.

The shooter took a deep breath and looked into Sarah Archer's room. The drapes had been pulled wide, and the shooter had a clear view, waiting quietly for the women to enter the room. In the dim lighting, the shooter could see Sarah Archer moving as one with her victim as they embraced and danced without music. Suddenly, the taller woman pushed back. Something had been said. The shooter's nerves tightened.

The woman known as "The Slasher" moved in closer and

slapped her victim violently with an open hand. Their body language, head movements, and lips signaled an argument. Just as quickly as it had begun, they both relaxed. Sarah moved in close again.

Gail Oppenheimer, the small town girl with the perfect figure, was about to become the tenth victim of an anomaly. Female serial killers were rare. Time was running out. The shooter was running out of chances to save one life by ending another.

The butt of the rifle was comfortable against the shooter's shoulder. The light was on in Sarah's apartment, making it easy to acquire the target.

A deep breath.

The shooter, the rifle, the bullet, the target all meshed together into one single entity.

The moment arrived.

Nothing moved except the shooter's right index finger.

Gail Oppenheimer had been helpless in the arms of a much stronger woman who was slowly bringing a razor to her throat. The blade flashed.

With no warning, it disappeared.

The grip of her attacker loosened.

And she was free.

Gail opened her eyes and gripped the back of a nearby chair. She was able to stand and for a few moments remain conscious. There was blood everywhere and what appeared to be bits of brain tissue and bone fragments on her shoulders and arms. The corpse's eyes were wide open from shock, and its mouth was twisted in a distorted painful looking grin. The side of the would-be killer's head was gone.

Gail began to tremble. A cold chill swept across her body. Then darkness swept over her.

The shooter watched through the Zeiss scope as Gail Oppenheimer's knees buckled and she dropped onto the lifeless body of her attacker. It had been a clean kill. One shot, not a moment late, and the life of a serial killer had ended.

Barrel, scope and stock slipped into the custom case that

appeared simply as an over-sized brief case. Matching luggage hid the gun case in what any observer would recognize as usual and customary gear for a traveler in the Great Smoky Mountains. It was time to move on. Spend the night on the Blue Ridge Parkway, not too far from Waynesville, an ambient mountain hamlet about twenty minutes West of Asheville.

The seclusion of the winding mountain road above the clouds would be a great escape all the way into Virginia. The view from the main dining room at the Mount Pisgah Inn's restaurant was devastating in its beauty.

PART ONE

It had been in the spring of 1976, May actually. Claudia Barry earned her master's degree at LSU in group dynamics that month. She had met a six foot, overweight man with a thick black mane in a dark, quiet bar on Highland Road that was now nameless in her mind. The conversation and the catfish po' boys were unforgettable.

"Perhaps, if I need a label, you could refer to me as 'the recruiter,'" he said. "You'll never see nor hear from me again. In reality, I don't exist. I'm not the assigner. I don't select the missions. I actually don't know for sure what you are agreeing to do for the party that will compensate you for your services. That entity will find you when and if they require your services again. There exists a labyrinth of layers and contacts complicated enough to assure mutual anonymity. With the exception of 'The Agreement' we discussed earlier, you're under no obligation to accept any assignment — but if you do, results will be required within the specified time allotted. From our meeting last year, it is my understanding that the assigner understands and has agreed to your stipulations. Would it be an appropriate deduction for me to make that you've kept your skills sharp?"

"You know my history and accomplishments. Not many shooters — regardless of sex — have the resume I've acquired. My vision is remarkable for any human. When I chose this career, it was obvious that I would never be in the limelight. I'll be happy to be just as anonymous as you." Claudia had resigned herself to anonymity even before the choice of professions. She had taken herself out of the fight for women's rights with the selection of careers. She couldn't attract attention to herself advocating any issue publicly and then hope to reach the upper echelons of her craft. She could, and did, find ways to make financial contributions to the cause. After her first few jobs, she had stashed away enough funds to live happily ever after — when and — if she ever retired.

After their meeting, over thirty years ago, he had disappeared forever. The Recruiter had excused himself and gone into the men's room. He had not come out. A five-foot-eight bald man who was skinny as a rail walked out alone and departed while attracting absolutely no attention whatsoever.

Chapter One

Before the barrel of her gun had cooled, Claudia Barry was risking the perils of a winding mountain road towards the Blue Ridge Parkway. It was not a good time to reflect upon the deeds of the previous few hours, the events that had put the shooter in this career and the constant need to project the image necessary to hide the truth. A thought that *it may be more dangerous for someone to be driving on these roads than to be in my cross-hairs* brought a smile as an oncoming vehicle straddled the double yellow line of a narrow two lane road.

The rising sun glared from behind the approaching vehicle. It was difficult to see. What a cruel twist of fate to get taken out by a distracted driver in the mountains, she thought. Gravity assisted acceleration shortened the allowable time for a quick glance at the radio dial, the CD player, or a cell phone. Even the most diligent driver would sometimes look up and realize their vehicle had strayed into the lane of oncoming traffic. It was not a good scenario in which to be if you sneezed several times consecutively.

It was time for Claudia to deal with her demons once and for all. The nightmares, the rationalizations, the endless questions that always seemed to be overridden by justifications. Tomorrow would be the right time. It had to be.

It was the reverie of a self-examination that would not happen any time soon.

The Smartphone pinged the arrival of an e-mail. The shooter pulled over at a scenic overlook on the Blue Ridge Parkway and checked the message.

Subject line: *Dinner reservations*. Without looking at the text, she sent back a reply that read, *No thx. Prevus engmnt.*

Within seconds, a text message arrived, *Call in — with precautions*. It wasn't an option. It was, however, a rare occurrence. Phone calls were unusual with the Clearing House.

Live conversations were done with disposable cell phones or satellite phones. It took her almost an hour to find a Walmart for the disposable phone. It was near Brevard, North Carolina, and just past Looking Glass Falls.

The Assigner at the Clearing House answered on the first ring, "I know you just finished a job," the voice said. "Remember our agreement. This is the job I've been holding for you – and you alone. It had to be assigned when the time was right. And the time is near."

"I remember. Now you're invoking our agreement. I'll certainly comply. Where's dinner?"

The agreement had been this: *Don't call me for an appointment someone else could keep. But if you call me personally, I'll know it's important and I'll be there.* This was the first time in almost twenty years that the Assigner had invoked the clause. It was the first time a succeeding job had come up with almost no delay. In the past, the shooter had seldom received more than one appointment a year. What was it now, thirty-seven jobs in thirty-four years? Had it really been thirty-four years?

Some assignments and some clients were memorable. Most of them were like the previous play in a sporting event. They had to be forgotten, and all available resources were needed to focus on the next one. The ability to compartmentalize was vital to keep from going crazy in an occupation where many others had cracked up after less than a dozen hits.

There had been one appointment that would remain unforgettable. It was the third one – the one that had made a name for Claudia Barry, forged a reputation and begun a streak of success seldom heard of in a line of work about which no one spoke. It was well suited to the personality and skills of the shooter. Few people enjoyed the privilege of such complete anonymity as to be invisible. Even fewer were as good at it.

The third man had shaken hands with destiny in the crush of a crowded reception and would never see the shooter again. The next morning, he was carried from the hotel in a body bag and, by dying, had given birth to memories and questions that haunted the shooter even now while entering the restaurant at the Mount Pisgah Inn. It was a favorite, and her preference was well known to the Clearing House.

"Yes, my usual table, please," Claudia said, and the

21

hostess led the way.

Claudia Barry's favorite table was near the middle group of windows and presented diners with a panoramic view of the Smoky Mountains from above many of them. Savoring the view was short-lived as her favorite server, "Mr. Joe," arrived, holding a glass filled with ice and liquor. It had a mint sprig on top.

"Tonight we have a special drink for you," he said. If it was special, that meant something would be under the coaster, and, sure enough, there was a two-inch-square sealed envelope concealed beneath the napkin.

"We have an anniversary coming up," Joe said in his congenial yet firm tone. "You've been dining with us now for twenty years."

Had it been that long? she asked herself.

"I must be getting old," Claudia replied aloud. "The months are flying by faster each year. And we've both added some gray."

"Well," said Joe, "what hasn't turned gray has turned loose," and they laughed together. Joe had a great sense of timing and knew it was time to walk away. His customer had more pressing matters than casual conversation – although they had shared more than casual conversation before.

I feel like I'm in a scene from Paladin, she thought to herself. *How long will they continue with these dramatics?* But there were other restaurants where assignments had been made: New York, Boston, and New Orleans.

After opening the envelope, she summoned Mr. Joe back to the table, "Can you see if there's a room available tonight at the Inn? I may be drinking more than usual and I'd rather not drive down the Parkway. And bring me another vodka/cran, please."

22

Chapter Two

Prior to March, 2012, the Heron Tower was the tallest building in London. That distinction had attracted the attention of Brian Farrell. The Shard London Bridge building was topped out that month. Workers placed a Christmas tree at the top to mark the completion of the steel skeleton. The new building took the designation as the tallest. The ITTA Corporation, a multinational conglomerate founded by and still under the watchful eye of Farrell, had moved its offices to the Heron building shortly after it opened in 2011.

Farrell was frustrated that he was no longer in the tallest building in London. The glass and steel tower was commonly known as "110 Bishopsgate." As a tribute to John Lennon, Farrell had purchased an original Andy Warhol portrait of the musician and used his influence to have it displayed near the aquarium in the lobby. The plaque read, "For the benefit of Mr. Kite."

Farrell was not a tall man, but neither was he short enough to suffer from the "Napoleon Complex." He could look the average height man right in the eye without adjusting the tilt of his head. Weekly rounds of golf kept his skin a healthy shade of light brown and his grip firm. He was proud of his handshake that conveyed a silent message of confidence and self-assuredness. He combed his hair straight back. That style accentuated a receding hairline. Combined with the thinning that could be expected of a man in his mid-fifties, Brian Farrell could have been a candidate for a hair transplant. But he was not that concerned with his appearance.

He once told a golfing partner, "I have a lot of faults, but vanity isn't one of them." His golfing partner that day had been an American powerbroker in the finance industry, a man who had amassed a sizeable fortune with shrewd investments. His name was Julian F. Thibaut. When Farrell made the vanity comment, Thibaut had smiled and shrugged his shoulders in a "whatever" gesture — but he would never forget it.

On the morning of Tuesday, July 5, 2011, Farrell was on the phone in his 46th floor office looking down on London. He turned to his associate, held his hand over the mouthpiece, and directed, "Get me Smitty on the line, please. He should be in New York with the ambassador. They had something going on at the United Nations this week."

"Yes Mr. Farrell," replied his assistant, Star Braun.

Moments later, as he was finishing the current call, she returned to let him know that his call was on line three.

"Smitty. What's happening in New York?" Farrell asked.

"The ambassador is pissed. I can't talk for very long. What do you have for me."

"Another appointment."

"Send me the info, and I'll assign it. When will you be in the States again?"

"Memphis in a few weeks. I'm donating a million dollars to the St. Jude's Children's Hospital. You know, the one Danny Thomas founded?"

"Yeah, I've heard of it. That should get you a few headlines. Maybe I'll see you on that trip. Meantime, consider this a done deal."

"I may be shaking the man's hand, so make damned sure you hire a straight shooter."

"Only the best." The line went dead.

As Farrell hung up the phone, Star asked, "Should I wire transfer the funds to Mr. Smith?"

"Yes, please. The usual amount."

"Which division?"

"Griffin's. He needed a bit of support for his banking operations. This should remove a road block for him that he didn't know about." And then to himself, Farrell mused, *And it will open a door for me.*

Farrell's assistant had worked with him for more than twenty years after starting out in the secretarial pool when she was in her twenties and still at the university. After wiring the funds, the tall slim blonde returned to his office, "Anything else?" She smiled, walked around behind his desk and stood near his chair.

Farrell looked into her Aryan blue eyes and placed his

24

hand on the inside of her right knee. Neither of them were uncomfortable with the familiar move.

She continued to smile.

He slowly moved his hand higher.

Chapter Three

Only the best. How many times had the assigner used that term in their numerous but brief conversations? Claudia Barry smiled to herself as she continued to enjoy her petite filet at the Mount Pisgah Inn restaurant. She ordered a glass of port to accompany the creme brulee for desert. She knew her limitations and seldom exceeded them. When she did, it was usually planned and arrangements were made to avoid driving. It was an intelligent, confident demeanor along with a youthful, mischievous appearance that made her attractive but not a head-turner. She worked hard at not standing out in a crowd. *Hell, I'm a grandmother who could make a longshoreman blush* she would say of herself. The penchant for self-effacing humor was instinctive and habitual.

Her efforts to blend in were assisted by her genes. At five-five, medium build, light brown hair, brown eyes and a penchant for conservative attire, she could disappear in a crowd in the blink of an eye. Unless you saw her in the gym, her physique remained an unknown asset. She was pleased with her aerobic prowess, and it was common for her to finish a grueling set when many could not. In workouts, machines were preferable to free weights as maintaining tone was more important than bulk. It was better to be flexible and solid than bulky and tight. She swam and worked on holding her breath at longer and longer intervals. Controlled breathing seemed like such a minor point, yet so many artists who relied on a sharp focus weren't conscious of how breathing moved the body.

It was such a surprise when she was discussing that exact point with cousin/photographer Wayne. He had done it at infrequent times over the years and always without conscious thought. After their conversation, it became an important point in his mental checklist before squeezing the shutter release — and his photography had improved as a result. In a bit of "quid pro quo," Wayne had shared his interest in Zen with Claudia. She embraced Zen and together with the awareness of breathing, her aim had improved. It was a significant event in her career and she

26

always gave Wayne the credit.

Exercise and diet had become so much a part of her routine that she seldom thought about it. She just did what she had to do. The biorhythms of her sixty-two year old body had fallen into sync. As often as possible she got deep body massages. She had learned how to stretch her skin as well as her muscles. With consistent effort a smooth healthy skin tone was possible. Another fortunate aspect of her genes was that her hair grew faster than average, but she preferred a short haircut. Once, she told a friend, "I've probably worn more wigs than Dolly Parton — but they weren't all blonde." and they'd laugh.

She was shocked that once last year she had been "carded" at a club. "Well it was dark," she had offered as an excuse, and would never admit to having had cosmetic surgery. Tans were nice but only when she needed one due to the location of an assignment. Lily white skin wasn't appropriate for a job in Miami. When she wore makeup, it was a pale shade of lip stick. When necessary for a job, she could match the efforts of Kevyn Aucoin or Bobbi Brown.

Controlling the aspects of her body and using certain muscles on purpose with unheard of control had made her an accomplished painter. Her balance, depth perception and small motor skills were remarkable.

"Honey come look at this." A stranger once said while walking by on the man-made sandy shore of Gulfport, Mississippi. Claudia was standing with the canvas at arm's length while she made delicate strokes with a long handled brush.

The husband caught up and hesitated. "May I?" he asked. After the approving nod, he stepped in closer for a good look. He smiled, shook his head in wonder and asked, "Do you do portraits?"

"No. I prefer sunsets and landscapes." *I find most people disgusting. Why would I want to paint them? So much of their behavior is offensive to me.*

He was about to speak again when she interrupted.

"I must decline," said the painter, anticipating his question with an uncanny accuracy. "If you have a sincere

27

interest in my work, you can see it on display at the Seaside Shop in Biloxi." It was more attention than she desired and an important lesson. She'd have to be more careful. It was significant enough to name: "The Gulfport Incident," and it had happened two years before she began her career as a professional assassin — at a time when she had already chosen to live in the shadows.

Claudia Barry had never known her father. Her mother had raised her back in an era when single parenting wasn't common. Most of the memories of her father had been created by stories from her mother and Grandpa O'Houlihan. When Claudia was old enough to begin talking, she tried to say "O'Houlihan". It came out "Hooligan." For the rest of his life, she would refer to him as "Granpa Hooligan" — and he loved it. No one had offered many details on how her birth father had died, simply that it was premature and that he shouldn't have gone so young nor so violently.

Cancer took her mother when Claudia was twelve, and so Grandpa became her second single parent. He had a knack for helping his protégé develop her accuracy with firearms, and it wasn't long before she could ignite a match stuck in the top of a fence post with a .22 rifle. They neatly put their bullets into the heads of squirrels to avoid destroying the meat. While hunting, she had expressed an almost obsessive interest in stealth. He taught her how to use camouflage and how to see through it.

When others found out what a great shot she had become, they were surprised to learn that she was no tomboy. Never one to flout her talents, Claudia became a self-styled recluse in junior college, and none of her Columbia, Missouri, high school friends ever knew that she had graduated from the University of Arkansas with a major in sociology and earned a master's degree at LSU in group dynamics. Disassociation from any childhood or teen acquaintances had become her first disappearing act.

Grandpa, a retired motorcycle mechanic, was a private man and either had the foresight or the negligence to forego a social security number for Claudia. Absence from the system had come in handy for her many times throughout her career.

28

Chapter Four

Julian F. Thibaut had not been born wealthy. He earned his fortune and was proud of his accomplishments. It had begun with a phenomenal sales career as a teenager in several multi-level marketing companies. Thibaut had parlayed his ability to inspire trust in others into a sales organization with national reach. At seventeen years of age he was leading a group of much older recruits, making friends, and building a network of contacts that would serve him well in the future.

His high school sales experience was followed by an enviable education at what he had always considered the flagship of the "Ivy League of the South," Vanderbilt University. He had grown up in Oxford — Mississippi, not England — in the shadows of Ole Miss and had looked down on the town and the university for as long as he could remember. He had an appropriate respect for the writings of William Faulkner and John Grisham but still felt that Vanderbilt was the place for him. A full academic scholarship took precedence over a possible athletic scholarship in golf. He had dazzled his contemporaries with his memory, but his real talent was his interpersonal skills. His sales experience had made him an insightful judge of character. He was adept at anticipating the behavior of others. Many times he had helped his friends develop talents they had not seen in themselves.

Even in college, his detractors said, "Julian never met a man he couldn't use." His friends knew him as someone who appreciated them for their strengths and had an uncanny way of helping them to exploit those strengths for their own benefit.

None of his classmates could understand why he majored in pure and applied English then applied for law school. No one knew why he never sat for the bar in spite of graduating with honors. Throughout his academic career, no one noticed that Julian also earned a degree in accounting and went back for an advanced degree in tax law.

Julian Thibaut had become a daring motorcycle rider in his teens. Few men of similar wealth were as cavalier about their physical safety except perhaps for the late Al Copeland of Popeye's Fried Chicken fame who raced speedboats on the high seas — along with Ross Perot.

His assets included a fleet of black Suburbans and a security detail of carefully selected guards, some of whom were former Secret Service agents.

Though well known among his financial peers and business associates, his income was unknown to the average man on the street. He did not stand out in a crowd. At six feet tall, his one hundred eighty-five pound frame made it easy for him to buy a suit off the rack. He was not pretty-boy attractive but handsome in the more classical sense, with chiseled features importing an aura of character. Julian Thibaut spent little time with stylists and wore his medium brown hair trimmed in a manner that worked as well in formal situations as in everyday life. It would have been fashionable enough in 1935, 1985, or 2011. He was careful of what he ate and was toned but not "buff."

Dining in public was not a concern. His security team would always be incognito at a nearby table. He often visited New York City on business. While there, Lido's in Hackensack, New Jersey, was a favorite for pizza. He liked a table in the back, in the dark, near the photos of Frank Sinatra, the Pope, and John F. Kennedy.

During his junior year at Vanderbilt, Julian had incorporated a business that would eventually become his financial empire, Double Entendre Investments. Using the national network of contacts he had established in high school, Julian focused on quadrupling the number of personal contacts that eventually led to international connections. Then, he began investing in stocks.

"I spread my assets around with interests in oil, real estate, technology, media and health care," he once told a reporter for *Barron's* — off the record. The woman had wanted an interview which he declined. "With my network and contacts, I know where my investments should be and I put them there well ahead of the curve," he continued. "By the time the stockbrokers are advising their clients how to invest in the latest trend, I've

30

already made my money and moved on."

The combination of money, business intuition, striking good looks and Southern charm made it easy for Julian to stay ahead of curves both financial and feminine. His experience on the highways made asphalt curves both challenging and inviting.

After college, he had moved his corporate offices to Maryland. Close to the Capital, and not inconvenient to New York. In his Baltimore office now, making plans, he said to his secretary, "Tell Chuck Martin that we're flying to Asheville next week. Make it Sunday. The helicopter is fine, I know he would rather fly it anyway. I've got a meeting in Atlanta on Friday and I want to ride the Dragon on the way."

"Yes, sir." replied Rosemary. "Will you be flying out of Knoxville to Atlanta?"

"Yes. After the Dragon, we'll ride on in to Tennessee."

"You really like riding that stretch of mountain road don't you?"

"It's very challenging for bike riders of any skill level. I'm riding my Harley this time."

"Do they still allow tractor-trailers?"

"No, they banned them a few years ago, at least in North Carolina. I think it was the same year they reduced the speed limit to thirty miles per hour. Maybe 2005?"

"I'll make sure Mr. Pointe and his security group knows about these plans."

Chapter Five

Astrid "Star" Braun, personal secretary to Brian Farrell opened the door and stepped into the 45th floor conference room in the London headquarters of the ITTA Corporation. Already seated and awaiting the arrival of Farrell were the heads of the four major divisions: Nigel Holmes, entertainment/media/sports; Martha Gore, health and environmental; Magruder Stone, educational media/software; and Griffin Challenger, of the financial division which oversees the ITTA interests in banking, insurance companies and stock brokerages. Also present was chief of staff, Warren Byrd, who usually chaired the meetings.

Today was exceptional. Farrell himself was scheduled to make a rare appearance and Ms. Braun announced, "Mr. Farrell is on a phone call with the Atlanta office and will be with us in a few moments. He asked that you be ready to comment on your reports. The meeting shouldn't take more than a half hour." Farrell believed in short meetings that began and ended on time. In this case, something had come up in the States that required his immediate attention. A typical staff meeting involved his comments and then those of each of the divisional heads. Their reports had been submitted in writing prior to the meeting and as he always insisted, "I can read. What I want from you in the meeting is any new or updated information not already in the report." The group was eager to see how Farrell would handle the report from Griffin Challenger. The last quarter had been dismal for finance — perhaps its worst in years. How would Farrell react and what would be Challenger's fate?

On the 46th floor of the Heron Tower, in his office, Farrell continued the telephone conversation: "You're kidding right?"

"No sir," came the reply. "Securing a membership into that group is more difficult than once expected."

Farrell was seated behind a six foot long library table that he used as a desk. Other than an old fashioned green ink blotter and the phone, the desk was bare. Farrell felt like a clean desk and a thin brief case — if any at all — conveyed his acquisition of power as well as anything physical in his environment, in addition to his attire. He always wore navy blue or dark gray suits with either red or bright yellow ties. "Every time we discuss this, there's always something new that pops up. I'm tired of the delays. You know I want in before the next U.S. Presidential election. Time is running out."

"It's hard to tell if we're going to make it by then."

"No it isn't. You're going to find a way. You have to make it happen. Now find out what it will take. You've got forty-eight hours," then Farrell slammed the phone down.

"Star. Are you out there?" he shouted towards the door.

In immediate response, the door opened and his secretary walked into his office. The slim Scandinavian had her long blonde hair in a bun revealing her neck. She had on a dark navy blue suit with a white collarless blouse revealing a mole that was seldom seen. At forty, she still turned heads and her stunning physical beauty often distracted the unfamiliar from noticing her competency both as a secretary and personal assistant.

Everyone thought in secret that she was having an affair with Farrell but were too afraid to voice their suspicions. Had they done so, they would have found that their speculations were common. Had they known the truth, they would have discovered that they were correct. Nevertheless, she was no dumb blonde and often disproved any concerns about her ability with an impressive display of some surprising business skill no one had expected.

She and Farrell were never guilty of any public display of affection and at work, even behind closed doors, kept up an impeccable image of professional behavior. "Yes sir," she replied, once inside the office.

"Someone in the 'Council' may have blackballed me. Contact our inside source and then call my sponsor. I want an update."

"Yes sir."

"Now, is the staff ready?"

"They're all in the conference room. Challenger seems upbeat and relaxed." She knew that Challenger had the most to

33

lose in today's meeting. "Everyone else is anticipating something big since you will be making an appearance."

"Do they think I should attend these meetings more often?"

"I'm not convinced that it matters. They enjoy your company and don't fear your presence. You've done a marvelous job of developing the relationship, if I may say so myself."

"I want a word with Warren after the meeting, then everyone's off to dinner. Will you be able to join us?"

"No, thank you. I have other plans. The reservations are set for the club at nine this evening. The chef was thrilled that you would be there yourself and she has prepared something special for the group."

"Here we go, then."

She held the door for him and the two of them walked down the hall to the lift.

Everyone stood with respect when the door opened. Farrell worked the room like a seasoned politician. It had been several months since he had seen most of them and it was Griffin Challenger's first meeting since his promotion. The CEO shook hands with everyone and added a hug for Martha Gore with an air kiss as well. When the pleasantries were finished, Farrell took his seat at the head of the table. Astrid Braun took the seat on the opposite end of the table and produced a note pad. Farrell began the meeting, turning his attention to Challenger.

"Griffin, you go first. I know you had a tough quarter and I want you to feel comfortable here with the group."

Challenger hesitated a moment. Farrell broke the ice with a comment and said with a smile, "Don't worry, I won't sneak up behind you and hit you in the head with a baseball bat." Everyone chuckled and Challenger relaxed.

"You're right, it has been a tough quarter for our units in the States. We're eliminating the insurance holdings that we cannot turn around. Several stock fund managers have been replaced and most of my attention the next quarter will be on our banking interests."

Farrell was reassuring and firm, "As a reminder to

34

everyone and of course to you, Griffin, I'm content to supply you with the resources and support to do your job. I leave you alone and expect you to reach the goals we've agreed on. Do you have the resources you need?"

"I'm confident that I've got the right people now," Challenger confirmed.

"How about funds? It takes money to make money."

"Fine."

"Political support? Legal? Do you need me to call one of my, er our judges?" Farrell had consciously included the Freudian slip for affect.

Challenger's right eyebrow raised for a moment, as if surprised. "I'll get back to you on that." One person in the room noticed. Star Braun had been watching his every reaction, his every move. When he had the chance to glance in her direction, he saw that she was watching him. He did not wonder why.

He had no way of knowing that she was pleased with his confidence and demeanor. She would give a favorable report to Farrell. Neither did Challenger know the dark, well—guarded secret in the room that everyone shared except him.

Farrell's mood changed. He looked Challenger in the eye and sharpened his tone, "Don't wait too late. If you can't bring me what I want in the next quarter, I'll find someone who can. Now you tell me what you need — anything — and it's yours. Do you understand? You need a verdict overturned? You want a specific vote in the U.S. Congress? Let me know in 24 hours."

"Yes sir." Challenger began to make notes in his pocket calendar and remained silent for the rest of the meeting.

Farrell continued, "Martha it looks like you're playing both sides of that global warming thing to our maximum benefit. We're making money either way."

"That is working out well. It would be great if our health division could avoid some pitfalls. We had to pull out of some diabetic drug studies and cancel research on that C.diff issue here in the U.K. A few negative headlines regarding deaths from those two decisions are going to be wiped out by next week's announcement of our advances in AIDS therapy and a possible

35

breakthrough with liver cancer."

"Thank you Martha." Farrell said with his trademark enthusiasm.

"Oh one more thing," Gore added, "That liver thing should get international headlines and become a big breaking story. We're pushing our research team for a Nobel."

"Excellent."

Farrell looked down the length of the table and said to Star, "Make a note for me to follow up on that Nobel campaign. We've had good results with two previous nominations. Let's see if we can make it three in a row."

"Yes sir," Star replied.

"Nigel, what's up with EMS?"

Farrell always enjoyed hearing Nigel's upper-class English accent and focused on the speaker. Holmes was in his late fifties. He was most senior of the current group of division managers. The others often sought his counsel.

"The Entertainment/Media/Sports division is set for a banner year. Recent surveys show that the sport of hockey is as popular in the States now as basketball. Soccer is making constant inroads in the public consciousness and more and more we see the media making the distinction by referring to football in the States as 'American football'. Our web-vision sites are gaining popularity against ESPN as well."

"What about endorsements?" Farrell asked.

"We severed ties with the athletes that bring bad press our way. Oh, by the way, thank you for the help with the newspapers and magazines on keeping that last incident as quiet as possible. *Sports Illustrated* buried the story of the most recent celeb endorsement we cancelled. The annual swimsuit edition is all the rage now and seems to be more popular than Jesus Christ."

Farrell let his emotions show again, "If that son-of-a-bitch gets in trouble or has one more negative headline associated with ITTA, his ass is grass."

"Sir, I believe you're picking up more Americanisms and I know of which player you speak. I can assure you, we'll have no more problems from him — or any of his ex-wives."

36

Now it was Magruder Stone's turn. Farrell looked in his direction and said, "You're up, Maggie."

Stone hated that nickname. "Thank you sir. The singular point I have to add to my written report is that the education/software division is monitoring the Internet censorship concerns that are all over the social media and the political landscape."

"What's our position on that?" Farrell asked.

"We're keeping our cards close to the vest until we can either clarify or influence events in our favor."

Farrell was pleased, "Stone, you've done a great job with your division. I want to speak to you tonight at dinner about a new project I've got in mind for the educational wing."

He nodded at Braun who took the cue and asked, "Any more questions or comments?" Another important meeting that had lasted less than thirty minutes was about to end.

No one responded so she continued, "Dinner will be at the Reform Club tonight. Cocktails at eight."

As the meeting broke up and everyone filed out, Griffin Challenger approached Nigel Holmes and as they shook hands asked, "May I have a moment of your time tonight over cocktails?"

Holmes was pleased at the request. He enjoyed his role as advisor and confidant of the other members of the management group. "Of course. I've been looking forward to a chat with you for some time. Yes, let's talk over drinks."

Part Two

There were two men in the life of Claudia Barry that had earned her respect and trust. The older of the two had been around for years, although they had not had the opportunity for much conversation since a lunch meeting in New Jersey in the fall of 1976. It had always been an occasional fleeting glance. Then one icy day in January of 1999, Claudia was dining alone at her favorite Irish pub, the Tir na nOg in downtown Manhattan, across from Penn Station when he walked up to her table.

"Claudia Barry?" the man asked. Yet he didn't seem too strange at all. She had been shocked that he knew her name, and yet she stood to meet him. It was instinct. Her manners were reflexive. She did not recognize him. She thought, "Do I know this man?" His six foot-seven frame towered over her. Her first impression was that he was older than she. The lines on his face could have been those acquired from experience, thought, and stress, rather than being written off as age-related. His hair was combed straight back with no part, and he wore wire-rimmed glasses. The frames reminded her of those she had seen in photos of men from the 1940's. The face reminded her of returning veterans from World War II. The nose, eyes, chin, jaw and cheeks were proportioned like God's architectural prototype for man. His lips seemed a bit too thin, but his smile was comforting.

"The name's , "Day-bear," and it's spelled..."

"D-e-b-e-r-t," she interrupted.

"Yes. And it's nice to meet someone who knows French. You never know these days."

"I spent several years in the Deep South — Louisiana. They speak a little French down there."

"I know." His voice was a rich baritone, almost bass, soft yet confident — and so masculine. He could have been the man of her dreams.

"How would you know that?", she asked.

"I've followed you for several years now," Debert said. "It isn't easy to keep track of your movements. But then you try so hard." He could see that she was becoming uneasy with that revelation. "Don't worry, I won't tell."

38

"I like your voice," she commented. "It's calming. There's something about the way you handle yourself and move about the room. You seem mysterious and, at the same time, charming."

There was a twinkle in his eye, and he smiled again.

"One day, you'll decide that you need someone to talk to," he said. "Someone you can rely upon. We can work out a way for you to let me know when you want to meet. We don't need to be as dramatic as Woodward, Bernstein and Deep Throat, or Mulder with his tape in the window. We'll think of something. I must be going now. If you wish, we can meet again, soon."

Across the dining room, near the bar, a water goblet hit the floor and shattered. A woman screamed. Claudia made a quick turn with her head and then dismissed it. When she resumed her position, the mystery man was gone. It seemed odd to her that during all the years since she had seen him last, he had never made contact until now. Could it be that in some way, his intuition had let him know that she was considering retirement? Yet, it seemed too far into the future to be considered now.

A few days later, she saw him walking ahead of her on the boardwalk in Atlantic City. She slowed her pace and followed him. After he had been seated at an outdoor table and was enjoying a drink, she approached him.

"Good afternoon, Mr. Debert," she said.

"Claudia, so nice to see you," as he stood and held a chair for her. "Have you been following me?"

She laughed and said, "I can assure you, our meeting today was a real coincidence, although you have been on my mind."

"In what way?" he asked,

"You suggested in Manhattan that I should trust you. You said you could be relied upon. You hinted that I might find in you, a confidant. Why?"

"Claudia, you've known me since you were six or seven years old. Don't you remember? You would often point me out to your grandfather and say, 'Look, Grandpa Hooligan, there's Mr.

39

Debert.'"

"You know what I called him."

"Why shouldn't I? I was always around."

They sat together in companionable silence while she thought. Finally, she said, "I'll wear a white scarf when I want to see you."

"What about after Labor Day?" he asked sincerely.

"That's for shoes," she said with a note of sarcasm.

The other man was John Hixon.

Chapter Six

Alone in her room at the Pisgah Inn, Claudia was absorbed in researching her next target. What appeared on her computer screen was hard to believe. When the list of transgressions got longer and longer and she began to recognize some of the events, she was impressed. Who would've thought? Farrell was so well insulated from the events that made him a mark for Claudia that she was surprised. After thirty years and all of her previous assignments, it was hard to surprise her. Even in his mid-fifties, the target was younger than she expected after reading about his accomplishments, as conflicted as they were.

She drew a line down the middle of a sheet of paper and started to list his actions and achievements. Good on the left and bad on the right.

Since 1990, he or his company had made donations every month to the Red Cross, Children's Miracle Network, and several relief organizations in the United Kingdom. At least once a year he got headlines with a six or seven figure donation to a high profile recipient. Last year it had been UNICEF. He was scheduled to visit a hospital in Tennessee soon with what promised to be a sizeable check.

He was a philanthropist.

The clearing house had always impressed Claudia with their access to information. Their research credited Farrell with varying degrees of involvement in the deaths of Benazir Bhutto, Andrew Breitbart, Vincent Foster and Ron Brown. There were at least a dozen others whose names were not familiar. She would look them up later.

He was a murderer.

She thought, *I'm surprised they didn't blame him for Michael Jackson, too.*

Brian Farrell was an astute businessman and a crook. He cursed like a stable boy and kept a copy of the *Holy Bible* on his night stand. He was close enough to British Ambassador William Farrell that he enjoyed diplomatic immunity. When she was done, neither side outweighed the other — in number. But, she asked

41

herself, *How much philanthropy does it take to counter a murder?* She raised one eyebrow.

Claudia's next target had worked without rest to avoid the media attention of his billionaire peers except for his high profile donations. Farrell had been so adept at avoiding the spotlight that most people in the world with similar net worth paid him little attention. He lived in a quiet but gated community tucked around a golf course. The security provided by the homeowners association was sufficient for him and his neighbors.

His residence was anything but ostentatious and blended in so well with the neighborhood that it was often missed by guests who came to his few parties. In the States, he drove his own car, a Chevrolet Impala, and frowned upon his friends who relied on chauffeurs.

The early morning golfers would have missed him by more than an hour. His next door neighbor saw the target leave early almost every morning — before sunrise. Those who knew anything about him appreciated his long hours and intense work ethic. What few of them realized was that he made the early morning drive from near Sparta, New Jersey, to a small private airport where he took a helicopter into New York City. Someone knew. This information was in the dossier that had arrived by e-mail the day after her phone conversation with the assigner.

While Claudia Barry was reviewing the material on her next assignment, Farrell was being interrupted by his private secretary, Star Braun, "PR is holding on line one. Sounds urgent."

"OK, she e-mailed me this morning. I was expecting her to call."

As Star turned and left the room, Farrell picked up the phone and demanded, "Don't tell me that son-of-a-bitch is dog fighting again."

At the same moment, Claudia Barry greeted the arrival of an old and trusted friend.

"Well good morning, Mr. Debert. I'm happy you could join me for breakfast."

"Thanks for the invite," Debert replied. "Let's enjoy the

weather and have something to eat. What do you say?"

"Wonderful. There's a quaint little soda shoppe at the foot of the mountain. It's the Juke Box Junction and they love Elvis and Marilyn Monroe there."

Chapter Seven

Debert held the door and Claudia led him into a fifties-style restaurant. Picture windows and skylights in the ceiling kept the rows of booths and tables well lit. Movie posters, signs and portraits of famous movie stars lined the walls. Monroe, Presley, Gable, Dean and the Three Stooges took the patrons back to another era while they enjoyed their sodas, hamburgers and fries. The booth on the end next to the back wall offered as much privacy as any seat in the house.

After they had placed their orders, Debert started the conversation.

"Tell me about this Mr. Hixon. How did you meet him?"

"Okay, here's the short version. Fayetteville. John Hixon and I were both undergrads at Arkansas. He was in law enforcement. I was a junior and it was the last semester for him — graduating senior. The FBI found him and made him a great offer. He minored in ballistics and had written several papers that were published. To this day, he can rattle off details and stats about a wide variety of ammunition. He can tell you the speed of the projectile, the rate of drop at varying distances from the target and how it changes with different loads of powder."

"He's learned his trade well," commented Debert.

"Add to that his independent study of psychology and he made a damned good investigator."

"Aha. Critical observation skills."

"He could analyze a crime scene and reconstruct the action as accurately as anyone."

"If he was so good, then why did he get out?"

"He retired — early, Claudia said. "Actually got a good deal from Uncle Sam. He hasn't told me the details yet. I do know that he left because he enjoyed seeing the perps receive their just desserts out in the real world. You know, save the taxpayers some money. It was frustrating for him when that didn't happen."

"Obviously the two of you are kindred spirits in that regard," said Debert.

Claudia continued, "Then he had to watch too many guilty criminals go free. After he left the agency, he disappeared into the Great Smoky Mountains."

"Vanished?" asked Debert.

"Well, not really. You know. Got off the radar — for good."

"Not too easy is it?"

"Not unless you've got the resources of the FBI. Or like me, never been on it."

"What do you mean, 'never been on it?'"

"Grandpa Hooligan never got me a Social Security number."

"As long as I've known you, I never knew that," remarked Debert.

"In the seventies, when I went to college, if you could produce the funds, they didn't ask for much more to accept you into college."

"I can see how not having a Social Security number would be important in keeping a low profile. How did you acquire a credit card? You do use credit cards, don't you?"

Laughing, Claudia said, "Yeah. I've got a whole deck of them, with addresses from Key West to New York City. John helped me with that, too."

"He does a lot for you, doesn't he?"

"Custom made equipment and ammo. He's a real craftsman when it comes to gunsmith arts. He loads a lot of my ammo by hand, too."

"You can't just walk into a Walmart and buy the guns and ammo you need for your work," Debert smiled.

"Another way to keep me invisible."

"One more question about Hixon. What drives him and how do you know you can trust him?"

Claudia thought for a moment. She wanted to say it just right. Wanted Debert to understand.

"Like me, he believes that to be successful in my craft," she paused for effect — "you must be convinced beyond the shadow of a doubt, that the ends we bring about will justify the

45

extreme means. He's earned my trust over the years with consistently doing and reacting exactly the way I expect — in every situation. He's dependable and loyal. Like you."

Chapter Eight

John Hixon met Claudia in Waynesville the morning after her breakfast with Debert at the soda shop. They drove to the end of the paved county road, then turned off onto a gravel lane that took them farther up to where the mountain touched the clouds. At the end of the gravel road, Hixon announced, "We have about an hour's walk from here to the cabin." Claudia smiled and thanked herself in silence for her dedication to the aerobic classes.

Their relationship was important to no one but them. Because of their life styles and personal choices, neither of them had many friends.

The people they called acquaintances knew one or the other of them. The occasional couple liked it that way. Wherever she hung her hat was home. He had deep roots in the mountains of Western North Carolina. Her profession demanded privacy. His personality made him a loner.

Claudia had experienced an adolescent excitement when Hixon invited her to visit his home. Now that it was near, she felt the charm and grace that love brings to a raw and unblemished natural world seldom visited by man. It was ideal for a loner. She wondered if Hixon ever read Thoreau.

Hixon pointed across a range of mountains and said with pride, "This part of North Carolina is where they filmed *Deliverance*. We know it as 'Little Canada.'"

"I was expecting to hear banjo music any moment."

John Hixon didn't laugh. He'd lived his entire life in these mountains - except for work - and he was loyal to his heritage.

"About two years ago, I ran two extension cords from that pole back there up to my place," he said. "One for the cabin and one for the barn. They power my saws, drill press, lathe and grinder. In the winter, I use them for my electric blanket."

"I bet you have some cold nights up here," she commented.

"I think I invented the expression, 'three dog night'," he replied with a laugh.

"The band?"

He shook his head, "When it's cold, I have to sleep with all three of my dogs to stay warm — especially if the electric blanket ain't workin'. I'm on the north side of the mountain, so around four in the afternoon, it starts coolin' off up here. This is about thirty-five hundred feet above sea level."

Claudia was charmed by the log cabin. "Tell me about your place. You built it didn't you?"

"Every log. Every notch. You sure 'bout this?"

"Yep." They made eye contact, and she smiled, "Every word."

In spite of his backwoods grammar, it was hard to hide the fact that he was well informed, educated and intelligent. Even though he sometimes chose to talk like one, John Hixon was no country hick. They had been hiking for almost a mile from the trail's end.

"Did that silencer do OK last time?"

"Fine." But she wanted to talk about his hidden home. "How many extension cords did it take to cover the distance?" she asked with a smile.

"Twenty-seven. The power company wouldn't come out any further than that pole. Scared of the bears, snakes and coyotes. Hell, I bring my shotgun when I walk through here most days — and always at night."

When they reached the clearing, she could see why they call the peaks around her the *Blue Ridge* mountains. Layer after layer of peaks cascaded into the horizon with various shades of blue. It reminded her of waves on the ocean. The cabin was a few yards away. She focused her camera on the distant peaks and was careful to avoid including the cabin in the frame. She respected his privacy. The safe harbor of a hidden retreat for herself was a dream. If there was any place on earth she wanted to keep hidden, it was Hixon's cabin. The sun was setting quickly. It would be cold soon. She stepped through the door and turned. His arms were open and she fell into his embrace with the carefree confidence of total freedom. No one would ever find them here. No one would ever know. No one else cared.

The smell of fresh coffee and bacon greeted her when she awoke the next morning.

John flashed her a smile from across the room. He was sipping coffee and cooking. "An electric skillet and Mr. Coffee stretch the limits of my cooking capabilities," he explained.

She pulled her legs up together and let them dangle off the side of the bed. Two of the three dogs moved and then readjusted themselves. She scratched their heads.

"I've never been able to stretch the limits of your other capabilities," she said, laughing out loud.

John Hixon had grown up in the mountains of western North Carolina. He had inherited twenty-seven acres of land high up in the clouds. He appreciated the culture here and the solitude. For him, it was never lonely. The animals let him know what was going on. Since the power company men left, no other human had been near. He knew the woods and the animals and their habits well. Some people thought he was an Indian. He felt like Davy Crockett.

Claudia loved all of the facets of his personality. She had learned to navigate crowded places and disappear quickly in urban areas. He taught her to do the same in the woods and the mountains. It was in Hixon's barn that he manufactured her custom made shooting gear.

"What do you do with this stuff that I make for you?" he had asked years ago.

"If I told you — I'd have to kill you." she had answered. She wasn't kidding.

He knew that even with their mutual trust, he was better off not knowing all her secrets.

He never asked again.

The space under the loft was high enough for him to stand under it without lowering his head. He stood six foot five and carried his two hundred and seventy-five pounds through the woods with the nimble ease of an experienced woodsman. His hands were larger than his face, yet he had precise small motor skills. He could tie a knot with one hand. He could reboot a computer with one hand. Years in the woods had sharpened his senses, but he still needed his reading glasses. The weather and exposure carved lines and wrinkles into his face like those of an older man, "But I'm still younger than you." he would tease her — because he wasn't. "I didn't shave, but I wore out a pair of fingernail scissors trimming my ear hairs when I heard you were coming to see me."

She laughed and said, "Next time, use a Weed Eater."

After breakfast, he unplugged the skillet and the coffeemaker. "I used the good china for you today. I like those paper plates with the shiny finish and the clear plastic forks."

She smiled, "We've got work to do, mister master machinist gunsmith. I need something special this time."

"Did I tell you I figured out a way to do the *heart attack* shot?"

"Keep talking."

"Well," he said, "you wanted a long distance shot that would penetrate clothing and Kevlar, then disintegrate inside the body, and not leave an exit wound. Right?"

"Yep. I want someone standing either near or in front of the target to think — at least for a minute, if not longer — that it was a heart attack."

"And you want the target to crumple where he stands. You don't need a ton of knockdown power."

"Uh-huh."

"Okay, here's what I've got. It's an idea for some custom ammo. I'll take the V-max payload from a 30-30 class cartridge — that's 150 grain load — and put it onto a high velocity 300 Winchester short magnum case. That will give you a shot that will leave a small entry wound, almost no noticeable hole in the clothing, mushroom out maybe even explode inside the chest cavity and not exit the body."

"So another person in the line of fire wouldn't be hurt. And at the same time, that other person would see my target grab his chest?"

"Right."

"And that works because..."

"We're taking a slug from a 30-30, with a speed of 2,300

feet per second, and putting it on a shell with enough gun powder to give it a faster speed of 3,200 fps."

"I'm with you. So, the faster speed would send it through the clothes without spreading out until it hits soft tissue?"

"Right. A clean kill. No blood — at least not for a few seconds."

"Ballistics?"

He broke into a big excited smile, "That's the best part."

Claudia couldn't help smiling, too. The enthusiasm was unbridled and contagious.

"My custom made *heart attack* bullet should mushroom and totally fragment in the first three to four inches of tissue. No exit wound, as we said. But now, get this. This is the really best part. No fragments large enough for ballistic identification."

The shooter was pleased. "Leaving no evidence is a nice fringe benefit. What would be the optimum range?"

"Four hundred yards."

"No loss of accuracy with that silencer you made for me a few years ago?"

"Nope. You had another request didn't you?"

"Right here in my case."

"Let me see those plans. Did you draw them up?"

"Yes."

He glanced away, deep in thought. His was a longer than usual pause, and tension began to build as the seconds passed.

After a few moments, John asked, "How soon do you need this stuff?"

"A month."

"I can do that. You up for about a four or five mile hike in the   mountains?"

"Sure. You know me. I work out a lot, and I've been looking forward to a tour of your mountain estate."

"Load up your pack and throw in a few bottles of water. You want a snack?"

"What are you taking?" she asked.

"A can of nuts, a couple bananas and a quart of Gatorade."

51

"Okay," she said, "Double it all and we'll be good. I'm bringing my new rifle. Would you carry my shotgun?"

They started off down into the valley just northwest of the cabin. The sun made the dew sparkle on the wildflowers, vines, and leaves of the trees along the trail. An inexperienced hiker would have never seen the trail, but John knew right where to step. Neither a rabbit nor a deer could have picked a course any better. She enjoyed the feel of the cool dew as it brushed her legs between her socks and hiking shorts. He stopped without warning and reached back for her.

He spoke in a soft stage whisper, "Check your vision now. Look over towards that rise, to the left of the broken pine."

About a hundred yards ahead was a balsam pine that had snapped about half way up. Maybe from snow last year. The top had fallen and hit the ground forming a triangle. About fifty yards to the left, she saw the slightest movement. She looked closer and focused her vision as the white tailed deer turned and looked back right at her. Their eyes met. Neither moved. A cross wind moved the top of the grass as John whispered, "I wasn't talking about the deer. Look about half way between the deer and us."

The breeze that had kept the tall grass moving, died. When the grass returned to its upright position she could see what he meant. Near the clearing, in the edge of the taller grass was a wild turkey. In spite of the contrasting colors, it was well hidden from view. She always learned more about illusions and hiding in plain sight on these trips out into the wild. It was impossible to avoid the animals on their route but more fun to see them first before being seen. They made their way down to the floor of the valley and then back up the other side.

The lunch was light and refreshing and they continued touring the Hixon estate. Two hours passed as they walked and then he announced, "We're about a mile from where we parked the Jeep yesterday afternoon." A moment later, they heard a car door slam.

"That sounded like it was right over there — only a few feet away."

John motioned for her to be quiet. He whispered, "It's the

52

acoustics of the mountains. I'm telling you it's a mile away, but someone found the Jeep."

"Who?"

"I don't know, but we'll find out, and they'll never know it."

"Any chance they'll find the extension cord?"

"They couldn't find it even if they knew it was there and were looking for it." Hixon was confident. The intruders were on his turf and he had the home-field advantage. Plus, they didn't know that he knew they were there.

Their pace quickened now, and he divided his attention between their route and their destination.

"Help me watch for activity around where they are," he told her. "Watch for birds. Squirrels. Any animal movement in response to theirs. There are more animals moving now. Sunset will be here in an hour or so. Bears will be out foraging."

After a few more yards, they stopped to listen. Movement. Something coming right towards them — and moving fast. It was a deer. A few yards to the left, a rabbit scampered past. "Coming towards us," he whispered.

Claudia followed him off their path and hid behind a huge pine. Nothing. "He stopped. Maybe went back."

The intruder had changed directions. Searching.

In fifteen minutes, Claudia and Hixon were hidden in the brush and dense foliage behind the pickup truck of their unwanted guest. Moments later, a short, almost fat man approached the truck. He had sweated through his khaki shirt from his laborious walking on the mountain. He leaned against the vehicle, removed a forest ranger hat and wiped his forehead and the top of his shaved dome. Claudia got several images of him with her combination binocular-digital camera. He drove away.

"He was an imposter, was he?" Claudia asked, confident that she was correct.

"I know all the rangers around here and he wasn't one of them. They're all too scared to come up here, just like the local police."

53

After a pause, Hixon asked, "So what do you make of our unexpected guest?"

Claudia thought for a moment and said, "Don't worry about him. I'll check out the plates and let you know. Did you notice that I took his picture?"

They finished their hike and arrived back at the cabin. Hixon began preparing supper.

"How about some squirrel stew?" he asked. She smiled. Her grandfather had been the last to prepare squirrel stew for her.

Chapter Nine

Forrest Cramer and Jerry Gregg were having breakfast in a diner in Atlanta, GA. They were on the personal security staff for Julian Thibaut, and they had been partners for almost two years. Their work shift would begin in just over an hour.

Gregg folded the *Atlanta Journal — Constitution* and laid it on the seat beside him and shook his head. "Another fanatic thinks the country is overrun with voting fraud."

"You aren't concerned?" asked his older partner, Cramer.

"Statistics show that voter fraud doesn't exist," replied Gregg.

"Don't you know that 87.6% of all statistics are made up?"

"I know that 100% of yours are," Gregg said with a smile.

"You should meet my old friend, Reverend George Clifford."

"Why?" asked Gregg.

"If you got to know him, or at least more about his operation, you might think differently about voter fraud."

"Keep talking."

"He's the pastor of a small church in Birmingham, Alabama. They may have forty to fifty families as members."

"What's that got to do with voting?" Gregg asked.

"Keep listening. Reverend Clifford's church owns a fleet of over thirty vans. Big ones. Eight to ten passengers." Cramer was smiling now.

"I've heard of churches having lots of vans, but not one that small."

"Election day for them is always a big day. Lots of food cooked and served and several hundred miles put on each vehicle."

"What's wrong with providing free transportation to voters on election day?" asked Gregg.

"Nothing — unless you're getting paid to do it — and paying the people to vote for a particular candidate."

"Is it illegal to pay people to vote for you?"

Cramer began laughing and stood up, "I'm going to the

jo—" and his head exploded. Gregg would later remember that he couldn't distinguish between the sound of the window shattering and the sound the bullet made when it hit Cramer.

Gregg reacted by rolling onto the floor and took an extra spin for distance. He landed on one knee with his pistol in one hand and his cell phone in the other. Ready to return fire and at the same time about to call in to the security office.

He surveyed the scene, eyes darting left and right, all around. The bullet had come through the plate glass window to his right and hit Cramer from what appeared to have been a level trajectory.

The shooter was still near — maybe in a vehicle.

He heard tires squeal. The vehicle was changing positions.

He was at risk.

A quick glance confirmed that he could do nothing for Cramer — *poor bastard*. Gregg slipped his cell phone into his jacket pocket and grabbed Cramer's wallet and the pistol he always carried in his shoulder holster.

A man had turned and covered his little boy in the booth next to Gregg.

The waitress that had just refilled their coffee cups was on the floor. The coffeepot she was carrying had shattered when it hit the tile and coffee was beginning to spread and mix with the blood now pooling around Cramer's open skull.

A teenaged girl sitting in the booth across the aisle vomited. Her companion had covered his head and was lying on the bench in the booth.

A middle-aged biker wearing a do-rag shouted, "What the fuck?"

Others dove for cover or ran for the door in panic-stricken confusion.

Gregg thought, *I've got to get out of here quick.*

He crawled on all fours as fast as he could — it reminded him of football drills in high school — and made his way into the kitchen. Once behind the swinging doors, he stood up and surveyed the scene from the diamond shaped window in one of

56

the doors. The dining room was an ant bed whose tranquility had been shattered by a lawn mower.

It had taken a few moments for most of the patrons in the diner to realize what had happened. An older woman with blue hair had panicked. She tried to hurry down the aisle past the corpse and slipped in the mixture of coffee, vomit and blood. The fall broke her hip and she shrieked loudly.

Her cries scared some of the other diners back into hiding.

Three construction workers got into a fistfight near the front door as they tried to force their way out of the diner.

The wait staff had disappeared. A battleship gray SUV circled the parking lot like a vulture seeking its prey. Without another target in sight, the driver turned into the morning traffic and was gone.

Gregg dialed a preset number on his cell phone. It was a line reserved for trouble. Pointe's assistant answered on the first ring and said, "You've been hit."

"Yes. How'd you know?"

"In the last five minutes, two other crews got hit, too. No time to call you. We'll bring you in as fast as possible using all safety precautions."

"I know what to do," Gregg replied, then disconnected. The safety precautions were meant to protect him and to maintain his cover. Pointe was adamant that an incident like this wouldn't be associated in the press with Thibaut or his company.

Jerry Gregg knew that simply because the SUV was gone, he wasn't out of danger. And there was no way he could use the car that he and Cramer had driven to the diner. He also had to escape before someone could make him.

He made a quick call and arranged for a cab to pick him up at a busy intersection two blocks away. He stepped behind a row of storage racks to the service entrance, opened the door and looked both ways.

Jerry Gregg was a man on the run.

He sprinted across the parking lot and into an alley. He jogged down the alley and composed himself. The cab was right on time and right where he had expected it to be. Six steps from

57

the alley at a normal but quickened pace got him into the cab. "Drive straight ahead, through this light and keep going," he said to the driver.

His cell phone rang. He pressed the button to connect the call but did not speak. The voice that came on said, "We're a few blocks behind you. Silver Volvo. Tell your driver to continue straight ahead. We'll pass you and do a 'bootlegger.' Tell him when he sees that to stop. Pay him now. When it happens, you jump outta the cab and into our car." The line went dead.

The Volvo had taken Gregg to a private airstrip near the 285 Loop, North of Atlanta, close to the Dunwoody area. He had stepped out of the Volvo and into a waiting Gulfstream for the short flight to Knoxville. It had been a quick trip — a little over an hour from the time of the shooting.

Gerald Pointe was debriefing Jerry Gregg in a secure office in a Knoxville industrial park warehouse. "I want to know everything you can remember. Have you two been to that diner before?"

"Yes. Often."

"Who waited on you?"

"Sally. She's been there since before we became regulars."

"Who was in the next booth?"

"A twenty something father and a little boy."

"Behind Cramer?"

"The booth was empty."

Pointe pressed on, "What about the booth across the aisle?"

"A teen couple. While I was grabbing Cramer's gun and wallet, she threw up."

"Other than Sally, did you recognize anyone in the diner? Another face you've seen there before?"

"No," Gregg was confident.

"Where did you park?"

"There's a line of trees near a side street. We parked in the shade."

"What vehicles were next to you?"

"A white Ford Explorer on one side and an old green

Dodge sedan on the other."

"Did you see the shooter's car earlier in the morning?"

"No."

Pointe's interrogation demeanor was calm and reassuring — almost hypnotic. He mirrored Gregg's posture, movements, and breathing patterns. They were in sync — body and mind — moving together in a somnambulistic trance. Gregg retold the scene, detail by detail. What he saw in his peripheral vision was now as clear as if it had been his primary focus.

"You're giving us great information, now, Gregg. Was the shooter in the passenger side or back seat?"

"He was in the back seat, behind the driver."

"While you were beginning your escape move, did you see if the shooter was trying for a shot at you?"

"No, sir. I did see the gun still up, but didn't know if he was trying for another shot or not."

"Fine, now, one more thing and we're done."

"Okay."

"What was the license plate number on the vehicle?"

"Don't know. The predominant color was green. Reminded me of those custom plates promoting the Smoky Mountains. I've seen lots of them in North Carolina."

"What was the first number after the letters?" Pointe coaxed.

"Eight. There was an eight after the letter 'B'."

"Can you remember any other details?" It was a shot in the dark, but he couldn't end without an open-ended question.

Gregg thought a minute and said, "Oh, yeah. The driver had a patch over one eye."

Pointe's response was calming, "You've had a stressful day. Go eat. You must be hungry by now."

They stood and walked out of the room together. Just outside, a woman who appeared to be about Gregg's age approached. Her black hair was cut in a classic "Bettie Page" style and she had a tattoo on her left shoulder, which was bare due to her halter top.

Pointe introduced them, "Jerry, this is Jennifer. She's one

59

of my assistants and I asked her to join you for dinner."

Part Three

Claudia Barry walked between the rows of books in the library of Hickman High in Columbia, Missouri. It was the last week of school. The summer of 1965 was about to begin. She had just completed her sophomore year and celebrated her sixteenth birthday — alone.

Claudia had been approved to work all summer as a volunteer at the main branch of the Boone County library. Her goal was to learn to use the library's resources to do research. By September, she had become proficient with the Dewey Decimal System, the Reader's Guide to Periodical Literature and the microfiche device.

In late August of the following summer, the head librarian, Mrs. Laird, came to the table where Claudia was working and asked, "After two summers of research, have you found what you were looking for?"

Claudia smiled and told a convincing lie, "I wasn't looking for anything in particular, but I have learned a lot about genealogy."

The librarian did not see the article Claudia had been reading from a 1952 New Orleans Times-Picayune. The headline read, "Mid-westerner killed in Garden District drug raid." Claudia had jotted down the name of the officer responsible. It was Emile Duplessis.

Ten years later, Duplessis had worked his way through the New Orleans bureaucracy to the position of co-chair of the city's Criminal Justice Committee. It was Ascension Sunday and he had attended the evening mass at the St. Louis Cathedral alone. As he left the service, a young man called out to him, "Mr. Duplessis. Please help me."

The kindly older gentleman found it hard to resist a personal call for help so he stepped eagerly into Pirate's Alley to offer his assistance to the young man in need. Perhaps he was feeling benevolent upon leaving the religious service.

They walked arm in arm several paces into the alley then the young man turned to his companion and said, "This is for Barry -- Clarence Barry. Remember him?"

61

Her disguise and make-shift silencer worked to perfection. The immoral cop and corrupt politician crumpled into a heap in the darkness of the alley. Claudia disappeared into the night and reemerged a few blocks over on Toulouse Street. She quickly made her way to Bourbon Street.

Anyone who noticed her now would see a twenty-something female in short shorts and a cut off Ohio State t-shirt.

The aroma on Bourbon Street was a combination of rotting garbage, beer, urine and vomit. Claudia was overcome by weakness. She held onto a light post to keep her balance. Then, her knees buckled and she made a contribution to the nauseating fragrance that tourists associate with the French Quarter.

Chapter Ten

A visit to her hotel room by Debert wasn't that unusual, but this one was unexpected. He seemed to have an agenda and shortly after pleasantries, Claudia found out.

"You're a murderer. Plain and simple." Debert was being blunt. She was accustomed to that from her friend.

"We've had this conversation before," replied Claudia.

"Yes, and we'll have some variation of it again, I'm certain." Debert pressed the issue. "You kill people for money. Then deny you do it for the money. You've got some deep dark desire to be Paul Kersey."

"Must I remind you once again that I saw *Death Wish* in '74? I was at LSU beginning my master's program. I saw it at the Varsity Theater outside the North gates to the campus — back when they actually showed movies there. Vigilantism is not my thing. And I'm quite at ease with the moral issues involved here."

"How can you be?" Debert exclaimed.

"Compartmentalization. Have you ever been in a submarine? I know you've seen photos or movies."

"Yes," Debert confessed. "That old television program, *The Silent Service*, was a favorite."

"My life is the same as being in a submarine."

"Go on..."

"That part of my life that as I refer to as "The Shooter" is sealed up in a compartment. Remember when the men in the sub move from one area to another they closed those heavy doors then spun a big wheel to seal the room?"

"Yes."

"Watertight, airtight. Like everyone, my life is made up of a number of roles that I must play. Not a single one of them has any room for doubt, apprehension or a lack of confidence. Sometimes I change roles several times a day. Sometimes, I stop in between roles. I stop to listen when I cannot hear a thing. There's always something there. In my case, changing roles often involves life or death situations."

"I guess it does." Debert was shaking his head in

frustrated wonder. "How do you seal up morals in different compartments? Isn't that a bit hypocritical? You sound like a psychopath."

"Listen. Here's my thoughts on that. Now, tell me if I'm wrong. Deep down, everyone is a little bit conservative. Everyone experiences times in their lives where situational ethics make them appear to be hypocrites — both to their observers and more importantly, to the person they see in the mirror. How can someone who does what I do live with themselves?"

"Isn't that how we started this conversation?"

"Don't distract me, I'm about to get warmed up. Would you like another glass of wine?"

"Thanks, I'm probably going to need it."

Claudia refilled their glasses then continued, "Here's one example. When I lived in Baton Rouge, I knew quite a few people, men in particular, who would profess their belief that abortion should be banned. Complete total ban in every situation. They'd brag about standing up in meetings of the Knights of Columbus and announce bold, confident proclamations of their beliefs. They were fond of using absolutes like 'always' and 'never'."

"It's good to see people stand firm with their convictions, don't you think?" asked Debert.

"Ah, yes, but listen to this. Find one of those men out of that environment and ask them in private, 'What if it were your wife or daughter that got raped by a retarded, homeless drug addict?' The expression on their face would change and then you'd see what I'm talking about when I say, 'situational ethics.'"

"Well..."

"I'm not done. That same concept applies in almost every area of life. Business, home life, social situations, recreation, entertainment and sports. Don't get me started on sports. Take a look at the skewed ethics of racism. Bear Bryant was one of the first coaches in the Southeastern Conference to go out and recruit Blacks to play football. Other schools soon followed suit. At LSU, they were no longer referred to as 'Blacks' but 'Tigers'."

64

"Now, back to business. Back in the early seventies, it took about seven years of research and millions of dollars to bring a new drug onto the market. Patent laws protected the original developer for seventeen years so they needed legal protection years before the first dose was sold. Now we're talking corporate espionage. You don't think people haven't died both from the espionage and from the developmental drugs? Someone's got to be held accountable. There are tons of crimes worldwide that no one is ever held accountable for. Oops. Sorry. I don't like to end sentences with prepositions — that one slipped. So, returning to 'Crime and Punishment 101.' Ever heard of Roger Bacon?"

"Sounds familiar, but I'm sure you'll tell me. Please continue."

"Roger Bacon was a 13th century English scientist who was the first to detail the process of making gunpowder."

"Right up your alley," Debert smiled. He knew she was about to take the upper hand in this debate.

"He was also a scholar, philosopher, and a Franciscan who studied mathematics and logic."

"Aha." shouted Debert. "I knew you'd find a way to bring logic and religion into this conversation," and he laughed out loud.

Smiling now, Claudia took a breath and kept on talking. "Bacon embraced a paradigm shift of belief systems that was beginning to rock the church and Europe. The previous dogma was that 'understanding can come only through belief.' Of course this supported the position of the church as the source of knowledge and understanding. Bacon and his fellow-travelers favored the exact opposite point of view — that belief can come only through understanding. Bacon questioned everything. He could distinguish between documentable proof and unsubstantiated statements of persuasion. He believed in precise writing and saying what one meant. He was imprisoned for his beliefs."

"And how does all this justify you having become a murderer?"

65

Claudia ignored the question and continued, "It's all about belief systems of both individuals and collections of individuals — cultures. Do you think that governments that use capital punishment are guilty of murder? Do you agree that regardless of the efficiency of the judicial system that some criminals guilty of capital offenses go free? That's where I come in."

"But you don't select the targets."

"No. I trust the assigner."

"Or whoever it is that decides who lives and who dies."

"With one exception, I'm confident that justice was served with every pull of my trigger."

"The third man."

"Yes. And he may well have deserved it. I'll never know. It's my one regret. I did that one for the money. I could have retired after that job — but I didn't."

"Why not?"

Claudia continued, "This is all sounding a bit 'preachy' but my career reminds me a bit of the Greek goddess, 'Nemesis'. Are you familiar with her?"

Debert thought for a moment searching for the correct word, "Rival. I'm most familiar with a nemesis as being a rival."

"Well that's one definition," Claudia continued. "Used as a proper noun, 'Nemesis' was the Greek god of retribution. She was considered by most scholars to have been a minor figure, but had a major effect as the courier of punishment — in particular for crimes that may have gone unpunished."

"Avenge not thyself. I shall repay saith the Lord." Debert was quoting scripture.

"Romans. I'm familiar with that verse," Claudia answered. "Another writer summed it up well, at least to my way of thinking. An English professor named Foster, writing about Sam Spade wrote, 'Someone not bound by rules if those rules get in the way of justice, who brings retribution with a touch of desolation.' A person I once knew told me I could be an avenging angel. I prefer to think of myself as a 'desolation angel.'"

Debert changed the mood with a smile and refilled their glasses. "You've invoked a 13th century convict, corporate greed, and a 20th century vigilante to justify your career. You expect me to believe all that bullshit?"

Claudia had to smile.

Debert continued, "You kill for two reasons: you believe you're meting out justice and you are paid a king's ransom. You're also rationalizing."

Claudia hesitated before replying. She broke the silence with a subdued smile then said, "And I'm damned good at it."

Chapter Eleven

Griffin Sullivan Challenger III would be considered by most ordinary people in the United States to be a privileged man. Perhaps such a person would be jealous, perhaps disdainful. The Challenger name was well known in all the right places in American aristocracy. His grandfather had started a law practice in New York City after emigrating from Wales in 1899. Four generations of Challenger men had finished at Yale and been members of Skull and Bones.

By the time Challenger got back to his room at the Strand Palace, it was almost five o'clock. He had chosen to stay overnight close to the meeting rather than return to his flat in Kingston upon Thames. He would be returning to New York City in a few days anyway. While making the perfunctory call to his wife, he untied his shoe laces, slipped off his shoes and loosened his necktie.

To no surprise, she was gone so he left a message rather than chase her down on her cell phone. She was too busy being in all the right places with all the right people doing all the right things to be interrupted with useless information about his career. He poured himself a neat scotch and sat at the snack bar with his notes from the meeting.

He had written more than he thought. With a few exceptions, everything he had written pertained to the others in the meeting. Nigel Holmes and Martha Gore were the Brits. He thought for a moment and wondered if Gore was a married name or not. Was it English? Stone and himself were both Americans, although Challenger's roots were in Wales. He had watched and listened to how they reacted and responded to each other and to Farrell.

Ah, Farrell. What an enigma. Why was the ITTA Corp domiciled in London when Farrell spent most of his time elsewhere? Of course, he had Warren Byrd in London and it seemed as if Ms. Braun spent a lot of time in London unless she was traveling with Farrell.

Offended by Farrell's obvious suggestion that he could

influence U.S. government and regulatory agencies with ease, Challenger marveled at his arrogance. Gore had sounded so nonchalant about the deaths associated with her division. He thought to himself, "Maybe I should test Mr. Farrell's will. How would Farrell react if I bluntly asked for an assassination? God, I hope I'm not turning into another Mitch McDeere."

There was a knock on the door. He was expecting a guest, but not so soon. He opened the door and found Star Braun, still in her business attire from the meeting. "Come in," he welcomed her with an extended hand. She took it with the firm grip of an avid tennis player and stepped into the room. "May I offer you a drink?" he continued.

"Yes, thank you. I'll have whatever you're having unless you have some cognac."

"Chivas Regal."

"That's fine. Thank you for agreeing to see me on such short notice."

"No problem."

"You handled yourself quite well this afternoon."

"That was my first meeting with the division heads. It seems as though it's time to produce."

"I heard you ask to speak with Nigel."

"Yes. Advice from a seasoned veteran is always valuable."

He motioned her to the sofa as he walked over to the bar. When he returned, she took the glass and held it up for a toast. The casual informality and assumed familiarity caught him off guard although it was a pleasant surprise. He hadn't been sure what to expect.

"To the next quarter," she said.

He echoed the toast and took a seat in the arm chair facing the sofa, more relaxed now and still wary. He had not had an opportunity to look at her before without interruption. For a few moments they sat in silence as each studied the other. His eyes took their time moving up from the slight cleft in her chin to full, perfectly-shaped lips, prominent cheekbones, and high forehead, all within the bounds of an oval face. Her complexion was pale

69

but not unhealthy. Her blonde eyebrows had a slight arch and the same color lashes framed the blue eyes that earlier had appeared so cold and penetrating.

"I've been looking forward to acquainting myself with everyone in the management group, but I hadn't expected that process to begin with you. To what do I owe the pleasure of this visit?"

She put her drink on the table between them with a slow deliberate motion, all the while maintaining eye contact. The steel blue eyes from the afternoon's meeting somehow seemed a bit softer now. Griffin Challenger was about to experience a secret that every other member of the management team had previously enjoyed. A dangerous secret that they all knew could end their careers, and possibly their lives as well — if they broke silence. With a simultaneous motion, she slipped off her heels and with both hands reached up behind her head to undo the bun. Her hair fell well past her shoulders with a shake of her head.

She said nothing to him and smiled.

Chapter Twelve

Claudia stood up, brought another bottle of wine to the coffee table and asked, "Ready to hear about the latest man in my life?"

Debert sighed and replied, "Sometimes I wish you didn't trust me so completely."

"His name is Brian Farrell. Ever heard of him?"

Debert put his hand to his chin and rubbed his cheeks with thumb and fingers while he searched his memory. "Hmmm....The ambassador to the U.N. for Great Britain is named Farrell. Any relationship?"

"Yes. You're up on current events I see. I'm still working on the details of how they are connected, but it's close enough that Farrell enjoys the diplomatic immunity of the ambassador's entourage."

"Diplomatic immunity. That's a rather open-ended acceptance of behavior, 'carte blanche', if you will, for dirty deeds."

"Yep. And you can bet that Farrell has taken full advantage of it."

"How?" Debert asked.

"I'll get back to that in a few minutes. First some background. He's chairman and CEO of the ITTA Corporation."

"Not familiar."

"But you've heard of some of their subsidiaries. It's a multinational headquartered in London. They have offices in Zurich, Cape Town, the Falkland Islands, and several in the States: New York, Atlanta, New Orleans, St. Petersburg, and San Francisco."

"Sounds weighted towards the states. No offices in D.C.?"

"Doesn't need an office there. He operates out of the embassy. Don't let the locations in the States fool you. San Francisco and St. Pete are for vacations. ITTA maintains a presence there as a front. They have a few people there but everything is funneled through them to London. Atlanta and Dallas are the active sites. Each city is home to two of ITTA's divisions that operate in the United States. The health & environmental and the Entertainment/Media/Sports divisions are both in Dallas. You've heard of EMS haven't you?"

"Who hasn't? In many cable markets in the Southeast, they were one of the first twenty-four hour stations available."

"Atlanta is home to the divisions that handle educational software and the financial group. The financial group has banking, insurance, stocks and bonds."

"They're into a bit of everything aren't they?"

"Not a day goes by that the ITTA Corp doesn't touch some aspect of daily living for most humans, especially in North America. Know how they built such an empire?"

"Are you about to tell me that the ITTA Corp is the epitome of legal, moral, and ethical behavior?"

Claudia smiled and raised her wine glass for a toast, "Vita bella."

Chapter Thirteen

Gerald Pointe was in his office back in Baltimore speaking on the phone with Jennifer. "What do you have for me?"

"For several weeks now, Gregg and Cramer had been having gut feelings that our security team had been compromised. They were concerned about three of the guys. With nothing but intuition and no hard evidence, they were reluctant to report."

"We've got evidence now. Who were the three?"

"Hill, Blane, and Sweeney."

"Hill and Blane are out. They died yesterday about the same time as Cramer. Anything else?"

"No, but Gregg thinks he's in love," Jessica sighed.

Just before disconnecting, Pointe said, "Sex after a stressful situation can do that."

He immediately dialed Gregg's cell phone.

"Gregg here."

Pointe wasted no time, "Three of our teams got hit yesterday. One was eliminated. The other two, including yours, lost a man each."

"Damn. Who.."

"I've got a group working on it. Your information was good."

"I'm glad I could help," replied Gregg. "What's next for me?" He feared for his position.

Pointe smiled, "You'll be on Thibaut's detail next week."

"You mean it?"

"You can ride can't you?"

"Yes sir. Started riding motorcycles in high school."

"That's good. We're riding the Dragon's Tail. Ever heard of it?"

"Isn't one end of it at Deal's Gap?"

Pointe was pleased that his minion was familiar with the location, "Yes, and the other end is in Tennessee."

Chapter Fourteen

Two days after Claudia Barry left Hixon's mountain redoubt, he woke at sunrise and slipped out of his log cabin. It wasn't easy slipping out without arousing the dogs, but if he could do that, few other animals would be aware of him either. This morning he traveled light. He had prepared his .22 semi-automatic pistol the night before. After cleaning and oiling it, he had attached a custom silencer — a duplicate of one he had made for Claudia. Instead of his usual route through the woods to the road, he took an alternate trail through thicker brush and trees. The cool morning air invigorated him and he breathed deep to savor the aroma of the woods.

Hixon had been warned by Mr. Jimmy about a possible visit from someone who would bring no good. He didn't have to wait long. It was the man that had appeared without warning the last day of Claudia's visit. The man that had impersonated a forest ranger stopped his truck, got out, and looked around to survey the setting.

Hixon reached out from behind the tree and with the muzzle of his pistol barely two inches from its target, fired two rounds into the skull of the intruder. Neither round exited the cranium but rather ricocheted several times within and caused death in less than a second.

By the time he hit the ground, John had begun slipping a garbage bag over his head and pulling the drawstrings tight. No need for a lot of blood on the ground. Hixon tossed the body into the back of the pickup truck as easily as if it had been a bag of leaves. Within an hour, the body was buried in the mountains and Hixon was busy changing the VIN on the engine block. Later that afternoon, he visited with Mr. Jimmy at the general store.

"Mr. Jimmy, you didn't see a pickup truck headin' up my road today did you?"

Mr. Jimmy screwed up his face, as if in deep thought, and replied, "Nope."

"Nobody but me been on that road in months," said Hixon.

"Uh-huh. So little traffic, I wonder why you got a road at all. It's always covered with leaves. It ain't last year's leaves, it's the leaves from the year before. You need something?"

"Yeah," said John, "you got any powder? I'm doing some reloading this evening."

A few days later, Mr. Jimmy waved at John Hixon as he was driving by. Hixon stopped and went inside the store.

"I got some mail for you. Went into Waynesville the other day. While I was there I got your mail."

As usual, Hixon tossed the mail onto the front seat of the truck. He never showed any anticipation nor eagerness to open it. Mr. Jimmy could keep secrets and lie better than anyone Hixon knew. And he ought to know. He knew something no one else knew. Mr. Jimmy was his father.

The shadows engulfed his cabin and Hixon lit the oil lamp. It was a lot cheaper than electricity. Today's mail had included three books from Amazon and a letter. *The Guns of August* and *Do Androids Dream of Electric Sheep?* had arrived along with *Shoot Low, Boys, They're Riding Shetland Ponies* confirming his diverse and eclectic literary interests.

For the next half hour he perused the books, read the summaries on the book jackets and then found homes for them in his book case.

The letter was a rarity. It had been handwritten. It was unusual for Claudia to write. She must have enjoyed her visit. It came as no surprise, knowing Claudia, that the text was brief: "Discovered the identity of our guest. Dangerous fellow. You'll know what to do."

Hixon smiled. It was about time to turn in. He would sleep well tonight. He blew across the top of the lamp to extinguish the flame.

He'd already done what he needed to do.

Part Four

On the morning of March 12, 1976, Claudia Barry arrived at the Faculty Club on the campus of LSU when they opened at ten-thirty for an early lunch. A quick bowl of Creole Gumbo and it would be off to meet with the chair of her master's program, Dr. Francis Thibaut.

She noticed a day old copy of the Times—Picayune on the table next to hers. The headline brought a smile and a surreal sense of pride. It read, "Emile Duplessis found dead of gunshot wound in Pirate's Alley." She knew she would never receive accolades for her accomplishment, but she was pleased to see her work recognized.

A few more weeks and she would have her degree. The few people who knew her well enough to engage in personal conversations had often asked what she would do with an advanced degree in group dynamics. Her favorite comeback was "Group therapy of course," and they would share a laugh. The reality was that her destiny had been shaped by the events of the previous thirty-six hours.

The door to her committee chair's office was ajar but she knocked anyway. Francis J. Thibaut, Ph.D. had been at LSU for over twenty-seven years and had never overseen a master's program for such an obscure subject -- the study of a system of behaviors and psychological processes occurring within and between social groups.

Claudia Barry would be his first in group dynamics and, he anticipated, his last of any kind before retirement. He took a certain degree of pride in guiding her through the program to a master's degree.

"Come on in," he said as he welcomed her in his slow Louisiana drawl.

She stepped inside his office and found his high-backed chair turned away from her. She sat down opposite the desk.

"So, how am I doing?" The voice came from behind her.

She smiled and turned around, but no one was there.

She turned back around to see Dr. Thibaut standing just inside the doorway.

76

"I guess I shouldn't have left the door open." she said and they both laughed.

"I can't remember how many times I've asked you how you got interested in group dynamics and how you got so good at appearing and disappearing, but I have to admit, it's been fun — and challenging for me to have worked with you through this program. As you know, it will be a first for LSU. You might be written up in a journal."

In a flash, her mood changed, "If it requires me dropping out of this program without finishing, I will, but I do NOT want any publicity. No recognition. I'd rather disappear now." She continued silently, to herself, the way my career seems to be heading, I have to stay off the radar.

"There's obviously a reason — a backstory — to your desire for privacy," he commented.

"I've been invited to interview for two business opportunities that I cannot talk about."

"The C.I.A. and the F.B.I.?"

"No comment."

"Okay, okay. I'll take care of it. I suppose you won't make an appearance at graduation?"

"No. You can send my diploma to my post office box if you would," she suggested.

"Like I said earlier, this project has made me work more than usual on a candidate's masters. Where did you find out about the work of Bandler and Grinder?"

"Don't you remember? I told you that I took a Dale Carnegie Course a few years back? Way before the need for privacy was important. I entered their instructor training afterwards, although I never taught."

"That's right, you did mention it before. Go ahead."

"I met an instructor trainer from California and he told me about their work. What they do involves therapy using a person's choice of words and body language. It's closely associated with group dynamics. Sometimes, the group only has two people. He's been a great help with locating resources. Have you ever noticed that I never sit directly in front of you? If you're

77

somewhat to my right, you are more likely to agree with me. He taught me that — and introduced me to the study of group dynamics."

Then she changed the subject, "To keep you updated, I'm almost finished with the two sections on my paper dealing with illusions and diversions. The professional show people in Vegas and the street performers in New York have been of great assistance. Once they found out why I wanted to meet them, they were receptive. How did you arrange a connection with them?"

"Friend of a friend," he said, paused "..of a friend, of a friend. Soon, I'd like to hear more about your experiences with those guys without having to wait on your thesis paper."

"I'll put that on my schedule for after my trip to New York," Claudia replied.

"I've been experimenting with some of your suggestions. You told me several months ago about the seating arrangements. Ever since, I always make sure my wife is seated to my right when we're discussing certain things."

"When I saw the two of you at the Faculty Club last week, her body language told me that it wasn't working," Claudia smiled.

"Of course, I didn't see you."

"Yes, you did. I waited on you."

He was surprised, "What?"

I told you I wanted to include a section on my paper about disguises. Well, it worked, didn't it?"

He shook his head, shrugged his shoulders in defeat and ended the meeting with a question, "When will you have the paper completed?"

"I'm flying to Boston tomorrow. I'll be working with a street mime for several days, then taking the train to New York. I'm interviewing more street performers and I've got a project planned that will test my skill with disguises. That should finish my field work and I'll type it up when I return. How about three weeks, a month tops?"

"I look forward to seeing you when you return."

78

Chapter Fifteen

Baltimore, MD was north enough for Julian Thibaut.

He had long since separated himself from many of the divisive attitudes and cultural incongruences of the Deep South, but he could not forsake his family heritage and locate his corporate offices north of the Mason-Dixon Line. He disdained most of what he knew about everything inside the Beltway. Thibaut did not talk slow. He did, however, take the time to caress each word. It was because of this habit that New Yorkers would say he had a Southern drawl.

Baltimore was north enough.

Thibaut had two visitors in his office and he was on the phone, unaware of the specifics of the conversation outside in his secretary's office. He was expecting his security chief, Gerald Pointe. Thibaut was as attuned to his personal staff as he was the nuances of the stock market. He knew that his secretary had an unrequited crush on Pointe.

"Erased any tapes lately, Rosemary?" Pointe loved to tease Thibaut's secretary, Rosemary Woods.

"How old were you when Nixon resigned?" she asked.

"My grandmother told me all I know about Nixon," he smirked.

"You're so full of it."

"How old were you?" Pointe asked, knowing the response that was coming.

"You shouldn't ask a woman about her age, Mr. Manners. What you should do is ask me out to dinner. But you never do," she said with a feigned frown. "Is there another woman? Do I have competition — or are you one of those guys that's married to his job?"

Before Pointe could respond, the door to the boss's office opened and out walked two women who would attract attention anywhere they went alone. Together, their appearance seemed to demand scrutiny — for the contrast alone. Pointe grabbed his glasses for a more focused view. With no conscious thought, the consummate Southern gentleman stood. The first woman must

79

have been close to his six feet in height. He didn't have to adjust his gaze to look her in the eye. She filled out her frame and her Armani business suit but was clearly not overweight. She was a brunette with dark brown eyes. Pointe always noticed eye color. There was a confident air to her demeanor as she strode through the room heading for the hall door.

Her companion was noticeably shorter, probably about five-foot five and much thinner. Skin-tight jeans and a thin cotton tank top accentuated her Kate Moss figure and revealed everything underneath. It was easy to discern that her hair was dyed as it was an unnatural shade of red with purple streaks. It must have been a foot long and was styled into a long tall Mohawk. She had several piercings on her face and a portion of a tattoo visible on her left forearm. Her eyes were blue, unless they appeared so because of contacts.

The door closed behind them as they left. Pointe turned to Woods and asked, "Audrey Hepburn and Wendy O. Williams?"

Before she could answer, the voice of their boss came across the intercom, "Miss Moneypenney, please send in Mr. Bond."

Woods smiled to Pointe and said, "Oh dear, he knows about us."

As Pointe returned the smile and went into Thibaut's office, he asked, "Who doesn't?"

"Good morning, Jerry. Have a seat," Thibaut was in a receptive but concerned mood.

Pointe began, "We're recouping after our losses last week. PR steered the media towards random unrelated shootings. Nothing that would link any of the victims to us."

"Is it who I think it is?"

"Maybe. I'm working on that."

"Why would they take out our security people if they weren't planning something against me personally?"

"Diversion. What I'm working on is what the diversion involves. It's possible that our organization isn't the end target at all. Could be someone else. Even though the media is saying one thing, our community knows about it. Every private security group, in particular those with a significant individual they guard, is at defcon one now. I'm waiting to hear back from contacts in both the FBI and the Treasury Department. When a hit like this goes down, it attracts as much attention as a relative winning the lottery."

"You think something bigger is going on?"

"Yes. I don't think JFK would have continued on to Dallas if several of the Secret Service teams had been hit a few days before."

"Maybe this is a message to people in my position to stay put?"

"So they'll know where you are."

"Then I'm a stationary target."

"Yes sir."

"I think it's something else. I think it's a message. Like the one we sent to Obama with the party crashers."

"That they can hit you just as easy."

"Yep. They want me to know that they can get to me. You remember that Obama reversed himself on the issue of troops to Afghanistan right after the party crasher thing? I wonder which issue is of concern to them with me?"

"Banking? Real estate? Some bill in Congress?" Pointe asked.

"Doesn't matter. It won't work. They should know that. Where do we stand with our personnel?"

"I've activated replacements from the reserves. You know we're in good shape there. We have candidates standing in line to work for us. This incident caught us unaware and it won't happen again."

"Anything else on the radar?"

"Not much. One minor event that I'm not sure is relevant to us or not."

"Why mention it?"

Pointe frowned and scratched the back of his head, "It may turn out to be something and I'll watch it. A private investigator posing as a forest ranger disappeared last week in North Carolina. Not a trace. I've got to find out who he was

81

working for and what he was researching."

"Whom."

Sensing that the meeting was about to end, Pointe brought up his last subject. "I've got our best riders ready for the trip next week and I've decided to go as well. In addition to you, we'll have six other bikes and two Suburbans as chase vehicles. Webster, who doubles as a security man is also a certified EMT. Three guys are down there now doing advance work — riding the route, visiting shops, stores, any rest stops along the way. We'll be ready."

The phone rang and as Pointe rose to leave, his boss said, "Thanks Jerry. I'm looking forward to the ride."

In the outer office, Pointe looked at Woods and said, "Well I'm about to ride a dragon's tail, but I won't be in China."

"Send me a postcard?" asked Rosemary Woods.

"From Atlanta."

"With love?" inquired Woods.

Chapter Sixteen

The Reform Club was one of London's oldest clubs. It was founded in 1836 and changed its policy to allow women in 1981. Located on the south side of Pall Mall, it began as a political haven but in the 21st century had earned a reputation for being a social club devoid of political preferences. A three-piece group provided engaging background music with classic jazz selections. They had opened their set with "Blue Rondo ala Turk." A few selections later, they accepted a request from an American woman and played "Take Five."

When Farrell and his party entered the lounge, the jazz group was playing "The Girl From Ipanema." Farrell loosened his steps, grabbed Martha Gore by the hand and began to samba. No one in the ITTA group had expected this. They suspected that Farrell had a more relaxed side and now they were seeing it. When the song was over there were smiles and applause all around. Gore had made an eye-catching display of her dance skills as well. Farrell thanked his dance partner with a deep bow and went to have a drink with his chief of staff, Warren Byrd. They stayed at the bar chatting and the rest of the group got a table across the floor from the bar.

"I was expecting Frank to be here," commented Byrd.

Frank Gravelle was ITTA's corporate attorney and commuted between London and Atlanta, sometimes as often as twice a week. He had been with Farrell since the first office for ITTA opened in the States.

"He's in Atlanta working overtime on securing a seat for me on the council."

Byrd cocked his head in a slow and contemplative motion. Farrell anticipated what was coming. "Brian, are you sure it's worth the effort? We've been focused on this for over a year now — and you seem to be obsessing over —"

Farrell interrupted him, "Warren, I'm not sure that you or Star or even Frank realizes how important this is, and can be, to ITTA."

"Can I be honest?"

"Of course you can. That's what I pay you for, even if we don't agree."

"Is this really as important as you say? Are you sure this isn't some ego thing?"

"Why do you ask?"

"I've softened my position on the issue since the tenth anniversary of September 11. And we've done pretty damned well without your being on the council."

"I can use the same argument to support my position. Think of how much more we can accomplish if I were sitting on that board of directors."

Byrd gave him a neutral facial expression.

"Warren, don't you see? These are the most powerful financial people in the world. Money talks. Money pulls the strings for everything else. We don't need to influence the elections in any country. The master money managers control everything that happens no matter who is in office."

"And you have Frank, personally working on that?"

"Yes."

"I'm sure Frank has one of his best connections working on Martha's legal problems. Death by diabetes and c.diff can't be swept under the rug."

"Name a hospital that hasn't had to deal with nosocomial infections. Tell Martha to open a new department focused on hospital-acquired infections. Nigel will support her with some reports and some editorials. He's got an impressive stable of editors that will write whatever he says. Diabetes is so common now, I'm surprised the American Centers for Disease Control hasn't declared it an epidemic. It might as well be as contagious as AIDS. Looks like you need another drink, I sure do."

Byrd listened intently, but his eyes were on Griffin Challenger, who had arrived moments after Farrell had taken the dance floor. Challenger motioned to Nigel Holmes.

Holmes excused himself from his group and joined Challenger.

"Thanks, Nigel. I appreciate your taking a moment to speak with me."

"I'm honored that you want my opinion," Holmes replied.

"I can help the boss. He wants on the council, doesn't he? How do I approach him?"

Holmes was caught off guard, blindsided by the fact that Challenger knew specifically what Farrell wanted in desperation, and could also help him achieve it. The unflappable Holmes took a moment to recover and after a few moments, leaned in closer to Challenger and whispered, "I'll take care of it for you." He then leaned back, looked around, and asked out loud, "When are you returning to New York?"

Warren Byrd had spent the afternoon in a marathon meeting with Farrell outlining events and issues on their schedule for the coming calendar year. 2013 had promise. Although Byrd was no more than three years older than Farrell, he had, to the surprise of many, become somewhat of a father figure to his younger boss.

Warren Byrd was now 67 years old and still worked fifty to fifty-five hour weeks. He sent text messages and e-mails at all hours. He was a taskmaster and expected his direct reports to answer his calls within four rings. Based in London, he had plunged headlong into his work with a dedication and resolve unlike ever before in his life after his wife of 37 years had died when American Airlines Flight 77 crashed into the Pentagon on September 11, 2001. He and his wife had never had children. With her gone, he threw frugality out the window. He wore custom tailored suits and shirts, Allen Edmond shoes, silk ties and diamond studded cuff links. For Byrd and those around him, there was no such thing as a "casual Friday" or any other day.

Years of constant work and layer upon layer of stress had not been kind to his body. Once he stood over six feet tall and now due to osteoporosis, he had a noticeable hump between his shoulder blades. When he held his head up, it forced his neck into a curve that reminded observers of a vulture. It was a label some gave him for his business style. His nose was long, thin, and pointed down at the end which did nothing to detract from the persona of Mr. Warren Byrd. His grayish brown hair was thinning now and he combed it straight back. What surprised people was his frequent smile that dominated his face and was contagious. It was so disarming that it aided him in negotiations and often made his victims open to attack. The texture, tone and color of the skin on his hands and fingers gave away the fact that he had never engaged in physical labor. He had never changed a tire or sparkplug and had never held a broom nor garden rake. Once a week, he had his fingernails manicured and received a fresh coat of clear polish.

The loss of his wife in such a high profile event had sparked his initial interest in gaining a seat for either himself or Farrell, or both, in one of the international groups that controlled world affairs. Now, he was beginning to wonder if it was worth the effort.

Farrell was concerned, "Warren, I've got to fly back to Atlanta for that meeting we discussed this afternoon. Were you planning on attending?"

"I've got a similar event in Geneva that week. It's possible, but it would be pushing it. Is Star going with you?"

"Yes, I want her there. She's got a good eye for reading people. She can be convincing, too."

"I'm sure you noticed Challenger over there talking to Nigel."

"Yes. I was expecting that. It's good for team building, don't you think?"

"Yes. Yes, of course. Do you think that Challenger is playing his trump card?"

"It does look as if he said something that surprised the old man."

From across the room, they could both see that the younger man had said something that caused the reserved elder statesman of the management group to react.

Griffin Challenger had attended Yale on a golf scholarship where he finished with double degrees in both forensic and management accounting. Standing next to Byrd now, Challenger looked younger and more athletic since he still played golf at least once a week. He had a tan with which he was pleased. His solid black hair fell down over his forehead. Thick

86

eyebrows and longer than usual, but still business-acceptable sideburns combined to frame his rugged, blemish-free face. His focus was frequently so intense that he forgot to smile. When he did, one was impressed with his almost perfect natural teeth. He was sipping his scotch and soda and talking nonstop.

"He may be rattling off the long list of names to Holmes, names of his friends from 'Skull and Bones'," mused Byrd. "Look at the contrast in the two men."

Farrell had picked up on it as well. He had not seen the two of them together in the eight months that Challenger had been with ITTA.

Holmes's stature was remarkable. He must be at least half a foot shorter and his years past fifty had added pounds to his frame and inches to his waistline.

Farrell remarked, "My god. They look like Abbott and Costello standing there together."

Byrd said, with a noteworthy tone of sympathy, "I'll have to mention to Holmes to avoid standing next to him in any group photos we might take." and then he faced Farrell and with a half smile, added, "I doubt that either of them would appreciate that characterization."

"How much longer until dinner is served?"

"I'll check." Then, turning his attention to two other members of their group, Byrd asked, "What could Maggie and Martha be talking about with such intensity?"

"Maybe he's trying to get into her pants."

"I thought she was gay."

"No. Maybe bisexual, but not gay."

"You seem rather sure of yourself, Mr. Farrell."

Farrell replied with a silent icy stare.

Chapter Seventeen

Gerald Pointe was asleep at the wheel of his black Suburban, parked at the Waffle House in Sylva, NC. It was five-thirty a.m. and John Hixon was due to arrive any minute. Pointe was tired and hungry after a night of driving, but happy to have arrived early enough catch a nap.

The deep roar of a diesel engine filtering through a worn out muffler shattered Pointe's rest and announced the arrival of his appointment.

John Hixon parked the World War II vintage deuce-and-a-half in the lot behind the restaurant and walked over to meet Pointe who was walking towards him. After introductions and pleasantries, Pointe motioned towards the behemoth vehicle and Hixon said, "I love that thing. Got it a year or two ago. When the electromagnetic pulse hits, I'll be able to drive when no one else can."

"You think that could actually happen?" asked Pointe.

"Anything can happen in a world where terrorists strike routinely. If it does, I'm ready. Most vehicles won't be able to crank. That thing will run and take me anywhere, in any weather."

"All wheel drive, huh?"

"Yep. All ten of 'em."

They had talked for a half hour over two All-American breakfasts and several cups of coffee, when Hixon began asking Pointe questions.

Pointe was frustrated. "Who's hiring who?"

"Whom," replied Hixon. "You've heard all about me and not sent me home yet, so I want to know about you. When did you get into the security business?"

"I grew up in a family of six in Birmingham, Alabama. Dad was in the steel mills and my mother was a schoolteacher. I was the oldest of the kids and took care of 'em — seems like all their lives. I was their protector. Beat the shit outta a lotta kids that was messin' with 'em."

"Do they still rely on you?" Hixon asked.

"They still call me now for advice."

"So how did you get into security for a rich guy?"

"No doubt, Mr. Thibaut is very wealthy. He's a modern day Horatio Alger. And he's a good man. Cares about people. Anyway, God blessed me with an incredible memory. I worked on the staff of a candidate for governor in Alabama. I could remember people's names and how he met them."

"You enjoyed that?" Hixon wanted to know.

"Yeah, it was great. I'd be right beside him briefing him on the next person he would shake hands with. So cool. 'This is Foster Hoffman from Gadsden. You met him at an alumni gathering in the fall of '98. His son, Brian, is at Bama on a scholarship you got for him. He's majoring in accounting. Ask him if Brian is going to join him in the family business.' I made him look damned good. Apparently not good enough, he didn't win the election."

"Interesting, but you got out of politics?"

"Got my degree in law enforcement at the University of Alabama - Birmingham. During my senior year, the CIA found me."

"Similar story here, except it was the FBI. I enjoyed my time there. Did you have any overseas assignments?"

Pointe hesitated a moment then answered, "I almost died from burns in a plane crash in Southeast Asia. Back in the states, while I was recovering, a mutual acquaintance put me in touch with Thibaut and the rest is history. Been with him for fifteen years."

Chapter Eighteen

The first time she had done it, the plan was to escape — something to help with the stress of anticipation. It soon became a part of the ritual leading up to the conclusion of each assignment. Claudia Barry took a vacation before changing roles and becoming "the shooter." She enjoyed being a tourist for a few days. Planning the trip became as important as planning the setting for the moment she pulled the trigger.

"Welcome to the Sandestin Hilton. Are you familiar with our property?" asked the well-tanned thirty-something man at the front desk.

"Yes. I've been here several times."

"Are you on vacation ma'am?"

"No."

"Let us know if you need anything."

Her luggage included her painting supplies and she looked forward to enjoying her other passion on the beach with the sound of the Gulf nearby. Whether it was crashing waves driven by strong winds or the soft splashes of easier tides, the repetition was settling for her — and reassuring.

Timing was everything and today was no different. Claudia had timed her arrival in the Florida Panhandle for late afternoon. She didn't enjoy being out in the sun when it was at its most intense. A casual stroll across the lobby to the elevators and up to her room left her plenty of time to unpack and lay out her things. In the room, she went straight to the balcony and checked the view. It was easy to see why this was called "The Emerald Coast." At first, she had believed that the clear green tint had come from the combination of the color of the water against the backdrop of the sugar-white sands beneath. Later, she discovered that it was the reflection of the light off of the micro algae. She could stand on the balcony and watch the waves for hours, but she had an agenda.

She turned away from the serenity of the ocean below, undressed and stretched out on the bed. It was great to be able to relax and rest with no pressures from the outside world. She thought, "If other people knew what I do for a living, would they think I had pressures from the outside world?" Then she allowed her thoughts to drift.

How had she become so involved with John Hixon?

What ever happened to her friend, Miss Lil, Dr. Thibaut's housekeeper?

Did any of her paintings sell last month? She needed to call the gallery in Biloxi.

Should she go to the islands anytime soon?

When she went for a jog later, would she go up the beach or down the beach first?

Her breathing became deeper and rhythmic and soon she was asleep.

When she awoke, she again went to the balcony and was pleased that the sun was still above the horizon. In fact, it was almost to the point that it could be gazed upon without fear of eye damage. She dressed right away and was off for a jog on the beach. She ran west. The sunset would be on her right as she returned. She kept her stride short and focused on the sand close enough to the water so that it was packed. Running in the dry deep sand was a chore. Her feet often splashed in the edge of the waves. She ran with her hands in fists, occasionally opening her fingers and shaking them out.

Splash, splash, double splash. She had company. She managed a quick and casual glance over her shoulder as the shadows began to close on her and discovered her fellow runner was a college type with blue University of Florida running shorts. He passed her like a seagull zipping past a turtle. It was time to reverse direction and head back to the hotel. The sun was on her right now and the ocean was beginning to settle into a smooth almost motionless surface.

An older woman was wading in the shallow waters holding the hem of her dress up above her knees to keep it dry. Tomorrow she would be back in her home town, working in her cubicle watching a computer monitor. Claudia thought, *that lonely woman represents the tragic end of all vacations*. The sun was a yellow ball with sharp, defined edges. The bottom edge sat on the horizon defined by the ocean. There wasn't a cloud in the sky. It reminded her of one of Miss Lil's stories. *Maybe that's why I paint so many sunsets.*

When she got back near the hotel, Claudia went to the seaside bar when it was about to close. She got a bottle of water and went back to the water's edge to watch the sunset alone with her memories of Hixon, Miss Lil, and the chairman of her master's program. *How much of her life had she spent alone? How much could she share with anyone else anyway?* As she was about to rise and leave, something caught her eye.

Almost invisible on the horizon was what appeared to be the bridge of a submarine as it took several minutes to submerge. Maybe a periscope would pierce the horizon, maybe not. She was surprised at how many sealed compartments she had to manage. She finished the water and walked back to the hotel.

The next morning, she was up with the sunrise. She liked to sleep with the drapes open and she was pleased with this room. She had stayed in this same room before and liked it because of the positioning of the windows and balcony. Morning and evening sunlight alternated to fill her room. After her morning run, she showered and went downstairs for breakfast. She would save a workout in the hotel fitness center for the afternoon when the sun was at its worst.

For now, she rented a pink Jeep and headed towards Destin. There were shops and shopping centers all along the beach road now — nothing like it had been on her first visit in 1972. She could have purchased what she wanted in the hotel, but wanted to escape for a while — away from the tourist traps and into the heart of the old town. After several stops she still had not found what she had envisioned. Then, after three more attempts and a referral from another shopper, she found it.

It was in an antique mall on the West side of Fort Walton Beach. It was a leather portfolio, somewhat smaller than a standard size sheet of paper. It would hold a writing tablet that measured six by nine inches. It was used, and worn by a lifetime of steady use. In spite of the wear and tear, the previous owners had taken care of it. The leather was soft and supple. The clasp

92

was secure and worked every time with no flaws. She held it in her left arm, like a schoolgirl would hold her books. She put her right arm around it and hugged it close to her chest. It was perfect. Then, on her way to the cashier's station, she saw something else that caught her eye. There was a display of antique fountain pens. These models all required bottles of ink. They were filled with a lever action and the sales person let her try several.

The lady behind the counter must have been in her late seventies. Her hair was a natural white rather than bottle blue.

Claudia thought to herself, *I bet she goes to the same beauty shop she's been going to on the same day of the week for over forty years.*

Her fingernails were shaped and painted with almost clear polish, the same as Claudia's.

Claudia asked, "Who does your nails? I need to have mine done while I'm in the area."

"I do them myself," the woman replied with a noticeable amout of pride in her voice. She was confident without being haughty and had a cheerful, helping demeanor. Claudia liked her immediately.

"Now that pen you selected is over $300, is that all right?"

"I expect for that price, it must have a gold nib?"

"Eighteen karat. This pen is a rare specimen. Discontinued in 1990. Once sold for over $500. It was made in Germany and has an iridium tip. Would you like to hear my 'official spiel?' I memorized it from their web site." She was beaming.

Claudia smiled, impressed with the older woman's salesmanship and memory, "Sure. Fire away!"

"These are writing instruments that reflect the personality of individuals with ageless tastes and classic preferences. After all, the spoken word lasts for just a breath. The written word lasts longer than life itself."

"Sold!" Claudia exclaimed. "And do you have any paper that will fit this portfolio?"

93

After her purchase, Claudia arrived back at the Sandestin Hilton a quarter past noon. The restaurant was busy and the indoor pool was jammed. The voices from the pool area filled the lobby.

In her room, she changed into a XXL Baltimore Colts football jersey she had purchased at Memorial Stadium in 1983. That was the last year the Colts had played in Baltimore before moving to Indianapolis and she had known one of the cheerleaders while an undergraduate. It became her favorite sleepwear the first night she had worn it and continued to be so after all these years. In addition to the nostalgia, it was damned comfortable — and it had no shoe company logo on it. Grandpa Hooligan had been a loyal Unitas fan and was saddened when the team left Baltimore.

She clipped and filed her nails into her preferred "sport" length and then added the flesh tinted polish, "Champagne" — her favorite color. Claudia then turned to her big project and the subject of her morning's shopping trip.

The pen performed like she had hoped. The ink was a light shade of blue and delivered an efficient flow through the nib and point onto the absorbent but smooth paper. She remembered previous attempts at using a fountain pen and had planned ahead. The ink had to flow and the paper couldn't be too rough. This combination was what she wanted. She began to write: *September 21, 2011.*

She thought to herself, *I can't believe that I haven't made any notes about my previous vacations! I bet there aren't many other tourists that kill more than time when they're on vacation.* Then she wrote, "This evening I'll begin a painting of the sunset."

Chapter Nineteen

Still waiting for dinner to begin at the Reform Club, Magruder Stone was speaking with Martha Gore, "I'm concerned about what you mentioned in the meeting today about deaths related to drug studies."

Gore's reply was cold and firm, "Don't be."

Stone continued to press, "I've got clients in education that were involved in diabetes studies that ended with no warning. Was that our doing?"

"What difference does it make if it was?"

"Well, if it was us, and they discover that, it would cause serious damage to ITTA's reputation in that community." Of the four divisions in ITTA Corporation, Stone was proud of the fact that his EMS division had both the best sales force and the most efficient technical support group. His division provided critical tech support and media influence for the other three divisions as well.

"When you've called me and asked for support, has my division ever said, 'Later' or 'we have other priorities?'"

"Don't try to put me over a barrel with your support."

"Wouldn't think of it. I'm simply asking for advance notice in case I need to be ready with a defense."

"You'll never have to defend your division because of something done by my division," Gore assured him.

Stone could see the boss approaching over Gore's shoulder, raised his glass in a mock toast and said, "Mr. Farrell is about to join us."

Gore held her glass and said so that Farrell could hear, "I'll drink to that. One son-of-a-bitch to another," and they both laughed.

"Martha, Magruder, good evening. Enjoying yourselves?"

Gore smiled and nodded her head while Stone spoke up, "Yes, sir — great change of pace. Where did you find that jazz group? They're great."

"Star knows someone in Nigel's entertainment group that found them. We've got a flock of four and five star reviews for

95

their latest CD on one of our web sites." He turned to Gore and smiled, "Martha would you excuse us, please? I'd like a few moments with our software man."

Gore smiled and shifted her voice to a lower register and mocked a newscaster, "Well he hasn't been too soft with me tonight." She and Farrell laughed and Stone offered a fake choking sound while turning around to walk with Farrell over to a secluded booth.

Warren Byrd looked at his watch, then around the room. He made eye contact with each of the other members of the dinner party and motioned them into their private room for dinner. Once assembled, he said, "Let me suggest that we all have another drink while Messrs. Farrell and Stone finish their conversation." He turned to the attendant who picked up on the request and went to the bar for another round of drinks.

Farrell had finished explaining to Stone what he wanted and Stone was concerned. "We've been working on that for several months now, sir."

"And I'm ready for some results," Farrell reminded.

"Our persistent adversary is still adversarial."

"I know. When will you be back in the states?"

"I'm planning a trip for later this year. And you?"

"I've got a meeting in Atlanta next month, mid-October. American football is one of my guilty pleasures. I've got tickets for the SEC Championship game in December so I won't be returning to London until after the first of the year."

They both sipped their drinks and sat in silence for a few moments.

Farrell broke the silence, "Thibaut is scheduled to attend the same meeting as I in Atlanta. It's this Friday. Maybe I can reason with him." To himself, Farrell thought, *If he's still alive, dammit.*

Stone took another sip of his drink and said with no emotion, "I saw a Tweet this afternoon that Thibaut's gone missing. Didn't arrive in Knoxville as expected. Motor car accident."

"Yeah, well, in the States, you aren't officially 'missing'

till you've been gone three days."

"Hmmmm. I see. Well it sounds as if he was riding some kind of dragon's ass in Tennessee."

Farrell relaxed as they stood to join the others for dinner, "Well there are a lot of asses in Tennessee. Some you want to fuck and some, well, you just run them for elected office," and they laughed as they walked toward the dining room.

Part Five

The Big Apple was abuzz with more than the usual summer vacation crowds in June of 1976. Claudia Barry walked up to the front desk at the Chelsea Hotel in New York City.

"May I help you?" the slender attendant asked. He was tall and thin and had an uncanny resemblance to Anthony Perkins.

Claudia thought to herself, "God, I hope his name isn't Bates."

"I have reservations."

They completed the paperwork and Norman gave her the key to her room. As she was turning to go to the elevator, he said, "Oh, Miss Berry."

"It's 'Barry.' Yes? What is it?"

"I almost forgot. There's a message for you. It came in a few hours before you arrived."

She had been on the train from Boston for over four hours — almost five. New York City was crowded with the usual summer vacationers multiplied this year by those arriving early in anticipation of the Bicentennial Celebration in a few weeks. It was a great time for her to be in town. She could disappear with ease in the throng. She unfolded the paper and saw the name and number. It was from Clothilde Theriot, Dr. Thibaut's secretary. She put the note into the notebook she had used on the train. She would return the call later. Their last meeting had been fine. She had detailed notes on what she needed for her thesis. What could he want now? It could wait.

She was tired. The train ride wasn't bad, but she hadn't rested much. When she walked out of Penn Station, she had joined a crowd on the steps of the post office. An a capella group had been performing soul songs and she had enjoyed it. When they finished, she had waited until the crowd dispersed and then spoken with several of the singers. She sat back down and made thorough notes from her conversation before walking to her hotel.

The next morning was the beginning of a personal challenge. She had two self-assignments. First, she wanted to

98

infiltrate the wait staff of the Waldorf Astoria Hotel, and for at least a few hours, become one of them — as a male. It was important for her thesis to show, how using deception, timing, and disguise, she could move in close to important people in spite of security. Second, her next goal would be to disappear from the premises undetected. Her effective use of group dynamics would be put to the test. She'd have to rely on an unplanned diversion to occur — unless she could come up with something on the spur of the minute.

The Chelsea was almost 30 blocks from the Waldorf Astoria. Claudia tipped the cab driver and walked through the main entrance. She held her head high and there was a noticeable spring in her step. There were hundreds of people jamming the lobby in anticipation of the breakfast meeting about to be hosted by Mayor Beame. He had arranged the affair to announce his successful endeavors to secure loans to bail out the city and avoid bankruptcy. President Ford had, in effect, told the city to "Drop dead" and Beame was pleased with his handling of the financing. Special guest at the breakfast was Representative Barbara Jordan from Houston, who in a few months would address the Democratic National Convention. Security would be tight.

Claudia entered a public restroom on the main floor near the ballroom where the breakfast meeting would occur. No one saw her exit. In one of the stalls, she changed from her business suit which consisted of a blouse, skirt and jacket into dark slacks and a white button down men's oxford shirt. She removed the brunette wig and shook her head letting her fresh cut hairstyle fall into place. Next the makeup was removed with cold cream to reveal her Gulf Coast tan. Her skin was smooth and clear and would pass for the fresh-shaved face of a man. She packed the clothes she had worn coming in and stepped out into the hallway. Claudia Barry disappeared into the crowd.

Down the hall, around the corner, and into the men's room and no one gave her a glance. The mayor and his party were arriving and the crowd was buzzing with energy and anticipation. By now, she found herself alone except for the

99

attendant. A ten dollar bill and a smile bought his inattention and poor memory. She wet her hair at the sink and applied a generous helping of styling gel. She combed it straight back and gave herself an approving look in the mirror.

The restroom attendant's name tag read, "Slim" and she addressed him that way with as deep a voice as she could muster. "Here's another ten, Mr. Slim. Where do the guys on the wait staff hang out?"

Fifteen minutes later, she was in the alley smoking a cigarette with three male waiters. No names were exchanged and the shortest of the group was talking.

"Yeah, Ford's no fucking help, so Beame had to do some serious sucking up to get us outta this jam."

A rather rotund member of the impromptu group added, "I don't give a shit. I want a check that don't bounce and some hope that they keep coming every two weeks — with some decent tips."

Claudia was relieved that "Mr. Rotund's" voice was softer and higher pitched than hers. She was hoping to avoid speaking at all when the one who seemed to be most diligent took a long drag, looked around at the group and said, "Let's go." She had passed the test. In conversation, it became clear that two of the others were new as well, employed for this breakfast. Once back inside, she grabbed a carafe full of fresh hot coffee and headed to the head table. She was comfortable and confident in her role. She had waited tables enough to pour coffee for anyone. Serve from the left, clear from the right. The guests at the head table knew not to raise their cup. Claudia filled their cups and worked her way down the table.

A step past the lectern, she leaned in to serve the next person and Mayor Beame himself turned and greeted her with a big smile. "Thank you." A wave of nausea overcame her and her knees buckled. He noticed and took her arm in his hand. "Are you OK?" he asked.

She smiled, regained her poise, and held on to the back of his chair for a moment. Without speaking, she nodded and smiled again and finished serving the head table. As she stepped down from the riser, she handed the near-empty coffee container to an approaching waiter, then everything went black.

"You managed to fool several people today," a voice crept into her consciousness. The exam lights hurt her eyes and she tried to sit up. "Relax," comforted the same voice.

"Where am I and how did I get here," she asked. Her arms were weak and her legs seemed too heavy.

"You're in the Medi-Quik walk-in clinic in Manhattan. Your friend out there brought you in." The nurse was kind and attempted to reassure her. "My name is Flo. Rest a few more minutes and I'll come back and take out the IV and then we have some paperwork to do. How long have you been pregnant?"

Claudia ignored the question and sat up on the exam table against the wishes of the attendant. Through the glass in the exam room, she could see Mr. Rotund sitting in the waiting area reading a shopworn Ladies Home Journal from what must have been 1959. As Flo was about to leave, Claudia touched her arm, cut her eyes toward Rotund, and said, "He doesn't know."

Flo smiled and left the room.

Twenty minutes later the nurse returned and asked, "Do you think you can stand?"

Claudia turned so that her legs hung off the side of the table, slid down until they touched the floor and raised herself to a standing position. The room wasn't spinning. She felt OK. No nausea.

"Let me lean against the table a few more minutes and I'll be all right," Claudia said with as much firmness in her voice as she could muster.

Then Flo walked out to the waiting area and told Rotund, "Your friend is awake now, would you like to go in?"

"Sure," he replied. Someone at the nurses' station dropped a clipboard and it hit a coffee cup on the way to the floor. He looked to see what was happening and then realized that normalcy would resume without his assistance.

He turned to the exam room and discovered it was empty.

All morning long, Norman, at the front desk had kept close watch on the lobby and its traffic watching for Claudia. She had received a second telephone call from that same woman with the Southern drawl that called him "honey." She had a strange name that could have come from Nova Scotia. Minutes before the midday foot traffic picked up he had seen a young man dressed as a service person that had disappeared before he could address him. No one that resembled Miss Barry had come through.

On the way back to the room, Claudia had picked up a Coke and now was relaxing on her bed taking a sip every now and then. She had been advised by an older pharmacist years ago that Coke syrup couldn't be beat for nausea. It tasted good and was beginning to take effect. She felt better and was gaining some strength.

"Pregnant?" she asked herself. "Damn".

The phone rang and she picked it up on the third ring, "Front desk here Miss Barry."

It was Norman. She had given him the slip earlier when she was in character.

"Yes, what is it?"

"You have another message from Baton Rouge. Mrs. Theriot again. This time she says it's urgent."

"I've got her number. Thanks."

Claudia hung up the phone, lay on her back with her forearm over her eyes and muttered out loud, "I'll rest my eyes a few minutes and then call..."

When she awoke, it was almost 10:30 p.m. She thought to herself, "It's late here. But it's 9:30 in Baton Rouge." She dialed the number and listened to the ringing sound.

"Thibaut residence," Miss Lil answered the phone like no other. A slow syrupy drawl filled with the kind of Southern charm an older black woman could impart. It was a lilting almost singsong announcement with several more syllables than necessary. Claudia had counted them many times and it was always at least seven and often eight or nine. "I wonder how many syllables she can include in the word, 'god'," Claudia had often mused.

"'Miss Lil,' this is Claudia Barry. Clothilde has been trying to reach me for over a day and I haven't been able to

102

return the call. I'm guessing she was calling for Dr. Thibaut."
*Claudia had met 'Miss Lil' a few weeks after Dr. Thibaut had
been assigned as her committee chair in the master's program.
Dr. Thibaut had invited Claudia over to his home on Cornell
Avenue several times. It was a block off Stanford and not far from
the Southern gate of the LSU campus.*

*Miss Lil was a matronly African-American woman who
had the skills to have been the housekeeper of an English manor
in the early 1900s. Miss Lil could have managed a dozen maids
and other servants. She had taken great pride in managing the
Thibaut residence ever since the good doctor had become
widowed. Once they had become acquainted, Miss Lil had taken
Claudia under her wing and become her surrogate mother.*

*"Miss Claudia, they were calling you because Doctor
Thibaut died day before yesterday. They're having the wake
tonight and the funeral is tomorrow morning."*

Chapter Twenty

Gerald Pointe was driving the black Suburban pulling a trailer with four motorcycles on board. They were on Interstate 40 heading west and had passed the last exit for Asheville.

"Where the hell is Deal's Gap?" Jerry Gregg asked his boss and travel companion.

"It's out in the woods, in the Great Smoky Mountains. It's on the edge of the national park and it's where the Dragon's Tail begins. Eleven miles of twists and turns. There are some hairpin turns and some of the turns have become so well known, they've named 'em. It's on the border between North Carolina and Tennessee. Since it's a national park, there aren't many access roads. No driveways or whatever. Makes a good area to ride. It's become world famous."

"What's the appeal? I mean, why drive for two hours just to drive more when you get there?"

Pointe laughed, "I thought you were a bike rider. A dedicated bike rider goes for the ride."

"Okay. I got it now."

"You'll love it. It's like a roller coaster with you at the controls. You ever been to the Smokies?"

"Once, when I was a kid. I was about ten years old. We went to Cherokee and saw that play they do in the open-air theater."

"*Unto These Hills.*"

"Yeah. That one. I don't remember much about it though."

"They reworked the production a few years ago. I haven't seen it since. It's about the Cherokee Nation and their forced relocation to Oklahoma."

Gregg was interested in the assignment, "What's our team going to be like?"

"You know a couple of the guys. Several are from the New York Office."

"Didn't you hire some new men?"

"We had to replace four. Yeah. The replacements are on

board, but none on this trip. I picked the men for this job based on their height and weight. We'll all be wearing the same gear, too. When we're standing around together with helmets on, no one will be able to pick out the boss."

"That's pretty cool."

"I'm paid to be cool," Pointe added with a smile. "We'll have four other guys on bikes with the boss and two chase vehicles. This and another identical one. Three backup bikes. Each SUV will have two of our security guys. We've got an EMT on board, a lawyer, and a mechanic who specializes in Harleys and sport bikes. Oh, and we've got a local dude who's a wilderness survivalist mountain man. He lives in the Smokies."

"Isn't this a bit overkill for an eleven mile ride?" Gregg was surprised with all the assets.

"The boss could make this trip alone and be fine. The attacks on our security teams changed everything. I tried to convince him to change his plans, but it's like talking to a brick wall. The eleven mile ride shouldn't be a big deal — other than it's slow. The speed limit used to be fifty, but a few years ago they lowered it to thirty. He's set to fly from Knoxville to Atlanta after the ride so we'll end up riding all the way into Knoxville. Do you have a preference between riding a Harley or a Suzuki?"

"Didn't you say the boss was going to be on a Harley?"

Pointe chuckled, "I didn't say."

"Well, I want to be on whatever the boss is riding. I want to be right up there next to him and you. Wouldn't it be a logical conclusion that you'll be riding next to him?"

"Yes. But why do you want to be up there?"

"Did I ever tell you about my football playing time?"

"You were a sharpshooter in college," Pointe remarked, confident with his memory.

"Yes, but I played football in high school."

"OK, tell me about it — and tell me what it's got to do with the question I asked you."

"I always liked to play on defense more than offense. When they let me, I'd play defensive end. I loved it out there. But in the early years, eighth grade, I was scared. By the time my

105

junior year rolled around, before every snap, I'd say to myself, *Man, I hope they come my way.* I wanted in on the action. I was confident in my skills and ability. It was like, *Bring it on.*"

"Now I see," Pointe made the connection.

Gregg continued, "When my senior year rolled around, I had gotten faster and bigger and it didn't matter if they came my way or not."

Pointe looked at him and raised an eyebrow as if to ask why.

"By that time, I was good enough they didn't want to come to my side — so I'd chase 'em down from the back side."

"What you're telling me is that even if you aren't on a Harley up front with the boss and me..."

"If something happens, I'll be in on it. Those Suzukis can fly."

They both laughed and then Pointe asked, "What will you be carrying on the ride?"

"I'm old school when it comes to sidearms. In some respects anyway. Ruger has a new 1911 semi-automatic .45 that I like. After a couple thousand rounds on the range, it's proven to be dependable. Then I've got a Sig P226 for my ankle, 9 mm. It's a bit big for that, but I figured we'll be on bikes and it should be easier to reach than the side arm."

"Even more so if you're not on a Harley," Pointe smiled.

"I like to carry a smaller pistol when I want more concealment. I've got a little Smith and Wesson that works well inside suit pants or jeans."

"Did you bring a rifle?"

"No sir. I did bring a sawed off shotgun though. Mossberg twelve gauge pump. I can rig it up for the bike and then I've got a leather holster for my thigh, too."

"You're gonna meet the boss in a few minutes. The landing strip in Bryson City isn't long enough for the Gulf Stream so he's flying in by helicopter. We're meeting him in a field a mile or so before we arrive at Deal's Gap."

"Cool." Gregg had been looking forward to this opportunity and had been thinking about what to say.

106

Anticipating his thoughts, Pointe assured, "Don't worry about what to say. Relax and be yourself. There won't be much time for bullshit."

"Got it."

After almost an hour had passed, Point pulled over onto the shoulder of NC Hwy 28. They got out and walked through a thinning area of the woods and found a clearing that was home to three buildings, one of which was clearly a barn. They walked out into the clearing past two driveways that led to two of the buildings. The distant "whop-whop" sound of a vintage Huey UH-1 become noticeable from the distant northwest. Thibaut and another security team had been in Gatlinburg, Tennessee the day before.

Thibaut had been a country music fan most of his life and had made it a point to meet and become friends with a number of Grand Ole Opry stars. He spent a lot of his leisure time in Gatlinburg and Pigeon Forge. Chuck Martin was at the controls and landed in the field long enough for his passenger to hit the ground walking at a brisk pace. Thibaut was already dressed in his riding clothes as the others would be soon. His motorcycle helmet was under his left arm and he extended his right hand as he approached Pointe and Gregg.

Gregg was impressed with the man's firm handshake. He jumped into the SUV in the seat behind Thibaut, Pointe was driving again and their boss broke the ice, "Martin is an amazing pilot. I think he could land that chopper on the 17th green at Augusta with no problems."

"He's meeting us in Knoxville?" Pointe asked.

"Yeah, and then it's on to Atlanta in the Gulfstream." Thibaut was enthusiastic. He turned around to include Jerry Gregg in the conversation, "Pointe here tells me you were a sharpshooter in college. You're an Aggie?"

"Yes sir."

"Have you ever killed a man?"

Gregg was surprised by the question and didn't answer right away.

Thibaut pressed, "Pointe didn't tell you that shooting

107

someone could be a part of your job?"

"Yes, he did — and no, I haven't shot anyone."

"I read your resume. You were a champion sharpshooter in college. Did you have any experience with quick drawing a pistol?"

"I was preparing to interview with the FBI and spent a lot of hours working on drawing a gun the way they do." Gregg was in more comfortable territory now, but still wary of the direction the conversation may go.

"I also saw the notes from your meeting with Pointe after your partner got shot. That was a first for you, too, wasn't it?"

"Yes. I'd never seen anyone shot in person. I had blood on my face afterwards and didn't realize it."

Thibaut turned on the charm and said, "I was impressed that you held your gun so steady afterwards."

"Thank you. I was surprised, too, when he told me to draw and fire." The morning of the shooting, as soon as Gregg had jumped into the Volvo, it had turned off the main street and into an alley. Pointe had lowered the window and ordered Gregg to shoot. Without hesitation and with killing accuracy, Gregg had hit the target — an odd colored brick in a wall — on his first and only shot. Windows went up and they joined the main stream of traffic once again.

Thibaut continued. "There was an article I read once, maybe an interview in *Playboy* with Al Michaels. He was talking about Michael Jordan's incredible vision. As I recall, he said they were sitting in Jordan's restaurant and Jordan was able to read the news crawl across the bottom of a television screen over 25 feet away. And it wasn't a wide screen. Amazing. How's your vision Gregg?"

"It may not be that good, but I see an ophthalmologist every year and my numbers haven't changed since I won those medals in college."

"Damn. A fast-draw with eagle vision." Thibaut punched Pointe on the shoulder and with a smile, said, "You know how to pick 'em, dude," and then thought to himself, *He better not choke when the chips are down.*

108

"Here we are," interrupted Pointe as he began to slow down and steer into the parking lot of the Deal's Gap Motorcycle Resort. The others were already there and beginning to unload the motorcycles from the trailer. It was clear and sunny, the skies a soft "Carolina blue" and a bit cool for a mid-September day. In addition to the "Pointe Team" assigned to the security detail, Gregg noticed a new face. The man was taller than the team and more muscular. He did not wear the black riding attire as the others and Pointe introduced him around.

"Mr. Thibaut, this is our local wilderness man, John Hixon."

After all the introductions, Pointe took over and it was back to work. "Here's the plan guys. Sweeney, you take one of the Yamahas and stay about a quarter mile ahead of us. Mr. Thibaut and I will be on Harleys followed by Gregg and Fanceca on the other two Yams. The guys in chase vehicles will be about a half mile or so behind. Hixon will be in his Jeep and go wherever he wants. We all have open mikes so stay in touch. Report any and everything. We want to give the boss an enjoyable, but safe ride today. Questions?"

He paused and had no responses, "Then let's saddle up."

John Hixon had grown weary of high tech communications long before he had retired. He laid his unit on the passenger's seat in his Jeep and finished taking the top down. The weather was good and he wanted an open-air drive today. By the time he had folded and tied down the soft top, the others had begun their ride. Sweeney had gone ahead, and the rest of them were almost out of sight when Hixon got into the driver's seat and turned the key.

Several years before, he had replaced the factory installed muffler with a glass pac "Flo-Master" and he was pleased with the result. The V-8 in his Jeep issued a pleasing sound to his ear through the replacement muffler. He smiled, let off the clutch, and pulled out onto U.S. 129 to follow at a safe distance behind the chase vehicles. He had never been fond of SUVs and had gotten his fill of Suburbans while in the FBI. His current employer for some reason thought it was cool for his security

109

detail to be in black Suburbans — like government services. At the thought of it, his only reaction was to shake his head.

About a half mile due north of the Deal's Gap Motorcycle Resort, the Dragon's Tail begins to earn its name. The road takes a ninety degree turn to the right for about the length of a football field and then does a 180 degree hairpin back to the left. If Hixon straightened out the first curve, he could pick up the journey without having to negotiate the hairpin. He had often considered doing that. If it were not for the thick growth of balsam pines, he would. As he approached the turn, he took his foot off the accelerator and hit the clutch to downshift. His Jeep was purring like a pack of firecrackers on the Fourth of July. It got louder when he stepped on the gas and he was anticipating that deep throaty sound when he heard something unexpected.

Chapter Twenty-one

He returned her smile.

Without warning his smile changed to a sneer and his eyebrows lowered. He stuck his thumbs into his ears, wiggled his fingers and stuck out his tongue. Then, as if to escape possible physical retribution, he turned and ran down the beach towards an approaching woman. Claudia was left alone again with her easel, a nearly completed sunset and a smile.

"I hope he wasn't bothering you," the woman called out as she approached.

"No. Not at all. In fact, we were discussing the differences in oil paint, water color and finger painting. This handsome young man was describing his last round of finger painting and what he used as a canvas," she laughed.

Mom smiled and said, "Yeah, he'll have nightmares about that experience for the rest of his life," and she laughed, too.

As the woman got nearer, she asked, "May I see your work?"

"Sure. Come on over."

"Some people don't like others looking over their shoulders."

"No problem. Take a look."

Claudia stood and stepped back from the easel and at that moment, she felt as though she had stepped back from the reality of her life. The thought of looking through the scope of a rifle and delivering what some would think of as justice to another human being was so remote as to seem impossible. *Could she have done that so many times in the past? Did those things happen? Could she do it again? Were those "day-tight compartments" impregnable to the present?* Standing here on a sugar beach in Florida with a stranger and her child watching the sun set, Claudia wondered what aspects of her own life the sun could be setting upon. Then, something happened for which she was not prepared. The woman's elbows were against her rib cage, her face in her hands and she was sobbing. The little boy tugged at her shirttail and asked, "What's wrong Mommie?"

Claudia, although shocked at the reaction, acting on instinct, reached for a tissue and offered it in silence by touching the woman's arm. What could have caused this woman to react this way to a painting of a sunset?

"I'm so sorry we interrupted your painting. First George, then me being all emotional."

"No worry. Please. I needed a break anyway."

The woman turned to the child and said, "Come on, George. Let's walk on down the beach a ways." Then to Claudia she said, "If you're still here when we return, maybe we can walk back to the hotel with you. I notice you have a towel there from the Hilton."

"That would be wonderful. I look forward to the visit," Claudia assured her.

As the two of them walked away, Claudia resumed her painting, this time from a standing position. What an inspiration. She added silhouettes of two figures walking hand in hand into the sunset to her painting. The sun, a huge orange-yellow ball behind them beneath a cloudless sky completed the composition. A few finishing touches were needed and she could add them back in her room. As soon as mother and child walked out of sight, Claudia packed up her gear and hurried along the water's edge back to the boardwalk from the beach up to the hotel.

Back in her room, she showered and then ordered dinner from room service. No need to risk further encounters with anyone who might want to become too chummy. While waiting on dinner she poured a glass of wine, opened her journal and began to write.

"September 21, 2011
8:47 p.m.

Surprised myself with how easy the painting went. Not complete, but close. A woman walking on the beach stopped and viewed my work — seeing it made her cry. I did not ask her why. Why would someone cry looking at a sunset? Maybe she feels the same way as Miss Lil. Maybe someone she loved is gone now." Then she asked herself, *Where is Farrell tonight? Will he be in Atlanta when I expect him? Where is Hixon — maybe in his mountain lair?"*

She had taken longer to write a few short lines than she planned and room service knocked.

"You're a Colts fan I see." The server noticed her jersey and was making small talk. He was a genteel, overweight but elegant, African-American man who seemed to be able to smile in any situation. Some hints of gray or white hair suggested that he might be a few years older than she.

"Put the cart over by the couch," she said. On his way out, she thanked him and handed him a ten.

"Thank you ma'am and Go Colts."

The filet mignon was cooked as she liked it. Last bit of pink in the middle had begun to fade and it was "melt-in-your-mouth" tender. The mushrooms and onions were a favorite side dish and the Mouton Cadet was the perfect complement. After dinner she resumed her writing.

"Baron Philippe de Rothschild once wrote, 'Wine, born, it lives, but die it does not, in Man it lives on.'

Should I care more about how he has lived? She wanted to add, *— or about how he dies?* but thought better of it. This journal could never become a confession. She continued, *What about me? Have I dealt with my pride?*

How good am I in a profession that will never earn me favorable headlines and the admiration of society?

When will I retire? I want to go out while I'm at the top of my game. When it comes to finances, I could have retired years ago. I need to make a trip to the islands soon — check on my accounts there.

"This journal writing thing is going nowhere," she said out loud to herself. "I've got pages full of questions and no answers. At least none I can put in writing."

She went to the desk and got out a piece of Sandestin Hilton letterhead and began to write, "Dear John." She paused and smiled. Then she chuckled out loud and walked over to the bar for more wine. She walked back to the couch and retrieved the paper and pen, moving her writing to the snack bar. "Don't worry, this is not a 'Dear John' letter. (ha ha) How would you

113

like to spend the winter with me in the Caymans? You can come to my retirement party." She didn't even sign her name. Before searching for an envelope, she cut off the letterhead. No sense leaving a trail.

Frustrated, she poured another glass of wine and turned on the television. The History Channel had another episode about Hitler and TBS had *Patton*. She thought to herself, *Isn't that John's favorite movie? And I've never seen it all the way through. Patton it is then.*

As Hixon had predicted, she enjoyed the opening monologue but before the scene where Patton met with the British knight to discuss air superiority, she had fallen asleep. When she woke up, it was 2:00 a.m. She turned off the television and walked over to the balcony. The sky was as cloudless as had been the afternoon. Despite the early morning hour, a gentle but hot breeze filled the air and felt good on her bare legs. The heavens were full of stars and the moon reflected off the silky smooth surface of the calm Gulf of Mexico. The thought of taking an early morning walk on the shore was appealing. Changing clothes and carrying a pistol were not, so she stayed on the balcony for a while longer.

Debert crossed her mind. Maybe he would arrive in time for breakfast tomorrow, or maybe lunch. The wine-induced sleep was past now and she was wide awake. She lay on the couch and found it difficult to relax her legs. She could not remember ever having been able to fall asleep when her legs were tense.

This had happened before. Every time, she had tossed and turned and debated over whether or not to take something to sleep. Seldom did she. It was rare for her to enjoy the luxury of no plans the next day. She had three more days on the coast before heading up to Atlanta. It would be the fourth visit to Atlanta in three months. The previous three trips had been to survey the area and plan her actions for the fourth and final trip on this assignment.

There were two possible places the event would occur and she was prepared for either. She had booked rooms in hotels across the street from both venues using different aliases. On her third visit, dressed as a postal worker, she had stepped off the distances involved, watched and made detailed notes of the wind patterns.

The assigner's information had narrowed the meeting down to either the Buckhead Club or The Commerce Club in downtown Atlanta. Either was fine for Claudia. There were ample locations within range and busy thoroughfares available for a convenient getaway after the assignment was complete. Over the next few weeks, she would change rental vehicles and identities several times and none would match the names on either of the reservations she had made in Atlanta. Confirmation of the final selection for the meeting would arrive by e-mail or text the day before, but she would keep both reservations. Front desk personnel would remember someone checking in at each. Her equipment would be arriving two days before the event in separate packages. The M-110 rife barrel was concealed in a walking cane. Hixon had insisted that she practice over and over until she could assemble the rifle and attach the scope in complete darkness. He had timed her and she experienced a great sense of accomplishment to be able to complete the task under two minutes.

If her plans worked out, assembly time would not be a significant factor. She should have both time and the benefit of light to prepare. She was tired of the repetition and the tenseness in her legs. She went to her medicine bag and looked through the choices: Flexeril, Ambien, Xanax and Dalmane. She settled on the muscle relaxer and warm milk. Instead of the couch, she got into bed and lay still in the fetal position on her left side. It was almost 4:00 a.m.

Four hours later, the maid knocked on the door before opening it and Claudia awoke in a groggy stupor. "Damn those pills." She said to herself as she reached for her pistol on the nightstand. Even if she didn't need it, she didn't want the woman from house cleaning to see it. She called out, "I'm sleeping in this morning. Could you come back later, please?"

The cleaning lady responded, "Yes ma'am. I'll be happy to. You want me to put the 'Do not disturb' sign out for you?"

115

"Yes, thank you."

Chapter Twenty-two

It was dark inside what appeared to Thibaut as a one-room house with a half loft. He had a pounding headache. The dim light was from a kerosene lamp that flickered from neglect. More light would have resulted from having more wick available. An adjustment was needed. Bright electric lights would have made it worse.

His host had been outside smoking a pipe. The distinctive aroma of vanilla flavored tobacco had drifted into the cabin with the night breeze.

Thibaut looked at the giant as Hixon entered the edge of the light from the lamp. There was disdain and more than a little fear in his voice as he asked, "Who the hell are you and where the fuck are we?"

"I'll be damned. You got a 'hell' and a 'fuck' in one question. And all this time I thought you were a gen-teel Suthun man."

Thibaut looked up at Hixon from under the ice pack on his head and shot him the bird.

"Why don't we start out by me telling you where you'd be if Mr. Pointe hadn't hired me."

Thibaut removed the ice pack and attempted to sit upright. He held onto the arm of the chair. He had no idea that the Morris chair he occupied was the favorite of his host and that he was the first guest to have that honor. Stability wasn't easy yet. Equilibrium was difficult to attain.

Hixon continued, "What's the last thing you remember hearing in your headset?"

"I have a headache that would register about an 8 on the Richter scale. Hmm...an explosion?"

Hixon yawned and stretched himself to his full height and in the small log cabin appeared taller than he was. He leaned over and tapped his pipe on the edge of the hearth and emptied the ashes.

"I doubt that. I didn't have on a headset and barely heard it myself. It wasn't that loud. Plenty of smoke and a big flash

117

from the gas tank exploding on Sweeney's bike."

"OK, what happened?" Thibaut stretched out his legs and leaned further back in the chair with his head back.

"I was about to make that 90 degree right turn and follow you guys when I saw the flash from the explosion. Something happened to the lead bike. I knew I could cut through the woods on foot and reach the scene quicker than if I went all the way around like y'all had to do. So I straightened out the curve and went as far as I could in the Jeep. I slipped through the woods without a sound, like I do when I'm hunting. I wasn't sure where the action was. A few yards before the clearing where I could see the road, there was gunfire. Sounded like a mix of rifles and pistols."

"A shootout?"

"Talk about. When I got to where I could see what was going on, all the bikes were on the ground. The guy on the other Harley and the two men who had been on the crotch rockets were all returning fire using their bikes for cover. You were laying on the pavement and not moving. I didn't know if you were dead or alive. I slipped in and started to drag you back into the woods. One of your guys moved to help me with you and took a bullet in the back. When your guys saw that, they stepped up the covering fire and I made it into the safety of the woods with you. Of course, I don't know who was hit or how bad it was. Oh, I did hear a helicopter later that day. Sounded like a Huey. It sounded like Vietnam."

"Thank you for being there. But how did you know it was me on the ground? We were all dressed alike."

"You're welcome. Being able to pick you out of the group was just one of the things you paid me for. My job to know which one you were. You know you're one lucky sumbitch."

"Other than the obvious, what do you mean?"

Hixon walked across the room and picked up Thibaut's motorcycle helmet.

"Here," he said as he handed it to Thibaut. "Check it out."

At first, he didn't see it. Then he rotated the head gear around into the light and there it was. It appeared as if someone had taken a cylinder shaped file and begun filing into the outside layer. The leading edge wasn't deep enough to say it was a hole, like a bullet entry, but it was close. Thibaut's attention was drawn to the opposite end of the graze. The further along the helmet, the wider the markings. The bullet had begun to mushroom upon impact. He looked up at Hixon.

"An inch or two deeper, and you'da been deadern' a doorknob. Now look across the bottom of the back of your helmet."

Thibaut found it then. A strip of white adhesive tape, reminiscent of the white paint on the back of officers helmets in the armed forces.

"I appreciate you rescuing me, but where are we?"

Hixon ignored the question and asked one himself, "Any idea who's trying to kill you?"

"You don't know me well enough for me to answer that."

"I know more about you than you think, but I understand. Well, at least we know it ain't Sweeney."

"I need some rest. Where's my cell phone?"

"Where would it be? When it was clear that you were alive but unconscious, I thought the safest thing for you would be to bring you here. I did check you for blood and make sure there were no hidden wounds. You're OK. But I didn't see a cell phone."

While Hixon was talking, Thibaut had been feeling his pockets and then remembered. He ripped open the Velcro pocket on the right leg of his riding pants and it was there. Crushed beyond use.

Thibaut's shoulders slumped. He put his elbows on his knees and rested his chin in his hands.

Hixon, ever the good host, asked, "You want to watch a movie?"

"I suppose a diversion, maybe escape for a few minutes wouldn't hurt. You got anything for a headache?"

"Yeah, I got some generic Tylenol. How about *Patton*? That's my favorite movie."

"Got anything else?"

119

"Four different versions of 'Blade Runner.' That's it. My collection of books is much bigger."

"*Patton.*"

Hixon began changing out the plugs in his power strip connecting the television and the VCR player while Thibaut adjusted the pillow behind his head and got comfortable in the Archie Bunker chair. "Tell me again how you got me here."

Hixon was fumbling with electric cords and trying to find the correct one to plug into the strip.

"Like I said, there was a lot of shootin' going on. From the direction your guys were returning fire, it looked like the shooters were all opposite of my position. So I dragged you back into the woods and into my Jeep. I had no way of knowing if your attackers knew you were gone. I got friends all through these mountains and there's a place I could hide the Jeep in the woods. You were out like a light. You took a real lick on your head when the bike went down. Anyway, after it got dark, it was easy to sneak you in here without anyone knowing.

"Here's one of my favorite parts, the opening speech. You know these are all Patton's words? But he didn't give this whole speech at one time. It's a collection of stuff he said but re-arranged for the movie."

Thibaut groaned.

"I love the part about shoveling shit in Louisiana." Hixon's enthusiasm wouldn't let him stop talking.

Thibaut's next response was a long, loud snore.

Hixon lowered the volume and watched the rest of the movie alone, which is how he always ended up watching *Patton.*

Thibaut woke up the next morning to the aroma of coffee perking and bacon frying. Hixon cut up the bacon into small pieces as it finished cooking and added the whipped eggs. Hixon noticed the movement and asked, "How do you like your coffee?"

Thibaut was much more alert and said with a smile, "Shaken — not stirred."

Hixon poured a cup of straight black coffee and thought to himself, *Well, at least he has a sense of humor.*

120

Hixon explained, "I've got enough electricity to run the coffeepot and the electric skillet without blowing a fuse. I've got some honey buns that have been right next to the coffeepot, so they're kinda warm. That's the closest thing I've got to bread."

Thibaut was busy eating. He had not eaten in almost twenty-four hours. "Whatever. It's fine — and I'm starving."

"I got some Ding Dongs and some Cajun trail mix, but the cupboard is almost bare. Need to go to the store soon."

Thibaut waved his fork and said, "Uh-huh," and kept eating.

Sensing that the time was right and his guest was able to think better, Hixon changed the subject, "You need to decide how long you want to stay under cover."

"More coffee, please."

"What are you going to do when you find out who's trying to kill you?"

"I'll annihilate them — before they do the same to me."

"Whoa. That's Rommel's line. You saw more of the movie than I thought."

"Not really, but as I said, I've seen it before. That's *my* favorite line of dialog."

After Thibaut had finished eating they walked outside. His host was waiting on him with a fresh load of tobacco in his pipe. It was one of his older, least expensive pipes and it was his favorite. The stem bore deep bite marks from weeks of use during the clearing of the site and building the cabin. Hixon waved his arm and with great pride, said, "Everything you can see belongs to me. Built the cabin myself with an axe and a chainsaw. I got twenty-seven acres here in these mountains and the opportunity to show them off is rare."

Thibaut took a breath and opened his mouth to ask "How much is it worth?" but something stopped him. Instead, he said, "You've got something many people long for and will never have. And I'm not talking about the land."

"Yeah, I know."

The two men who seemed to have little in common, yet made companions by a finesse of fate, stood and admired the

121

one-acre pond in the valley below Hixon's redoubt. It was a smooth and clear mirror reflecting the beauty of the mountains in the early morning light. Later, a gentle breeze added ripples to the surface but when the sun found clear skies above the balsam pines, a painful glare obstructed the view.

Unexpected events had forced the cooperation of opposing personalities. As they stood there admiring their surroundings, each man questioned how they would relate to each other. Would they become friends? Would they bond and force themselves to tolerate the other for the duration of their respective missions? What events did tomorrow hold that would require these men to cooperate in order to protect one — and maybe both of their lives? Hixon said, "I call this place, 'Tranquility Base'." Deep in the valley, a mourning dove cooed.

"What day is it?"

"It's Wednesday. The shootout happened on Monday. Don't tell me you're gonna have amnesia. Don't involve me in a soap opera."

"I'm due in Atlanta on Friday."

"And if you don't show up?"

"My staff knows how to cover for me. No one would miss me." He was lying and Hixon knew it.

"No doubt your staff could cover, but you run in big circles."

"You have no idea."

Hixon laughed, "I read *Captains and the Kings*."

Thibaut didn't react.

"And..." Hixon paused for effect, "I've seen every episode of *The X Files*, twice. My favorite two episodes were the one with the insurance salesman and the one where the CSM shot JFK."

"Oh god."

"I ain't in the Bilderbergers, but I can make you appear whenever and wherever you want."

"Now I guess you'll tell me that I can't escape this mountain hideout without your help."

"Which way is north?" Hixon taunted.

122

Thibaut was quick to reply, "The more relevant question is, 'Which way to Atlanta?'

Chapter Twenty-three

Claudia Barry had been sitting alone in a breakfast nook near the lobby of the Sandestin Hilton, scanning a copy of *The Walton Sun*, waiting on her friend to arrive. She had chosen a white scarf to complete her outfit.

"You got my message," she exclaimed with a smile as he approached her table.

"Yes, I did, thank you for the invitation." Debert was wearing Bermuda shorts, a black tee shirt under a colorful Hawaiian shirt and a wide-brim straw hat. The tropical shirt with orange background was unbuttoned to show off the image on his tee. It was a white dagger with a skull positioned where the handle met the blade.

"So happy you could join me for breakfast. How have you been?"

"I've been fine. Sort of expecting a call. Is this your typical pre-assignment vacation?"

"Yes. You know me well, don't you?" His attire got her attention.

"What's up with the choice of shirts?"

"The dagger bothers you?"

"I'm not sure..." she hesitated wondering what Debert was up to. "Is he mocking me — or is this some dark metaphor?" she asked herself.

Debert assumed a dignified frown, lowered his eyebrows and intoned, "You remember from your study of history, that in medieval times, before the age of printing, events were often documented with marks on the handles of knives."

"Mmmmm.....that does ring a bell," Claudia remembered. "And this shirt with a skull at the junction of the blade, handle, and guard?"

Debert smiled, "Well I have no idea how many skulls, or notches on your gun you might have, but I thought one would represent what you do in addition to all of them in toto."

Then he added, "It doesn't mean I approve of what you do, but I accept the fact that I can't change it." Then he added,

"And you seem to do well at it."

Claudia looked him in the eye and said, "You know I've had my own moments of doubt. I'm probably better at compartmentalizing than anything that I do."

"Did you notice the design on my outer shirt?"

Then it hit her and she burst out laughing.

"Oh my god. Hula girls. It's covered with hula girls in grass skirts and leis." With the combination of the dagger and the dancers, he was paying homage to her being a woman in a deadly profession and she appreciated it.

"I may see some hula girls soon." she blurted out.

"Oh? Going to the islands — after the assignment is complete?"

"Let's order and talk while we eat."

"I'll settle for coffee. Skipping breakfast this morning."

"I'm having a big one. I hope you don't mind that I ordered before you arrived."

"No problem. You know that. What's on your mind?"

"Several things. First, something curious. I've spent several late afternoons on the beach painting the sunset."

"You've got some great work on canvas. One day, I'd like to own one."

"One day, I'll give you one — a signed original — one of a kind. Anyway, a couple of evenings ago I was painting on the beach. A woman and her little boy walked by. He was way out ahead of her and was chatting me up when she arrived. When she looked at my painting, she started crying."

"Why do you suppose she started crying?" Debert asked.

"That's what I was going to ask you."

"Well, did you ask her?"

"No. I didn't want to either prolong nor deepen the pain."

"How can you be so sure it was pain?"

"She was sobbing. Her body language screamed 'pain,' not joy or happiness."

"Then, we'll never know. Tell me, how did you react and what does it all mean to you?"

"It blindsided me. Wasn't expecting that," Claudia

revealed. She took a sip of black coffee, held the cup in both hands in front of her face and thought for a moment.

"I couldn't think of anything to say. I felt so....aaah, so useless or inadequate."

"How could you be 'useless' if you created a piece of art that would elicit such a dramatic reaction?"

She shrugged her shoulders and Debert continued, "Don't you realize that there are millions of artists out there," he waved his hand in a sweeping motion, "who would die to see their work prompt such a reaction? They're doing what they do, paint, photograph, sculpt, whatever, desperately seeking such a response."

"I guess I remember the reviews and comments on my work that complained of a lack of emotional connect."

"That's bullshit. Whoever said that doesn't know what they're talking about. You should ignore the critics."

"But I've often felt that myself. Sometimes I feel cold and heartless. Maybe that's what makes it easy for me to have an emotional disconnect from my work. For some reason, it's always been easy to seal events and people and devastating emotions into one of those day-tight compartments."

Debert thought for a moment, raised his eyebrows and almost smiled, "Knowing that — at least in the case of this sunset — your work can evoke emotional responses, how does that make you feel?"

"Oh, so now you're a psychologist?" Claudia laughed.

"Well..."

"Ok, I felt several things. Vindicated for one. It was with some degree of satisfaction that I got to experience firsthand an incident where someone had an emotional reaction to my art."

"Is that all?" Debert wanted to hear more, push her closer to what her conscience was saying or feeling, maybe open one of those doors with a question mark on it.

"No, of course, there's always more. Afterwards, I thought more about the process of painting, that piece in particular. It came to me the next day as I continued painting. It took a couple more sessions to finish. But that second day, while

I was detailing the foreground, it occurred to me that while painting the major portion of the scene, I must have zoned out. Something. Another disconnect? I can't recall a single moment of actual painting after I got started. I used a three inch brush to do the background sky and beach — to apply the major color tones on the canvas. Then something happened. It was like I was in a trance. Then the little boy walked up and we started talking. I looked at my watch and almost two hours had passed. I don't know where that painting came from."

"It's obvious. It came from within yourself. No wonder an observer would respond with emotion," Debert offered.

"Something else I have experienced. In the days since this happened, I've felt an omnipresent aura, an incredible sense of anticipation of good things to come."

A moment of silence took center stage as both Claudia and Mr. Debert contemplated her premonition. She took a few more bites and a sip of coffee.

"Would you say that you feel at peace with yourself?"

"Yes, that's a good way to describe it."

"Anything special happen to bring this on?"

"You'll probably dismiss it as 'justification' or 'rationalization,' but I've come to terms with why I stay in this line of work," she paused for effect.

"Go ahead."

"Someone else selects the target. They must have a reason. Before the Internet, I'd spend hours in libraries and devouring newspapers. I got pretty good with in-depth research. With every assignment, I've always been able to document the selection with my own research."

"As being someone who...what's that they say in the South?"

"He needed killin.'"

"Are you familiar with the Latin word, 'palatin'? From that word evolved the present day 'paladin.'"

"A soldier of fortune?"

"More specifically, 'a knight without armor.'"

"A knight?"

"Yes. There was a group of them in the Eighth century affiliated with Charlemagne. Didn't you take world history in college?"

"Yes, some of this is starting to sound familiar. I remember hearing Charlemagne's name frequently," Claudia confirmed.

"Charlemagne's gang was often referred to as the 'Twelve Peers' and were considered to have been the foremost warriors of his court."

"I liked the reference to the knight without armor."

"These knights were all men."

"There was one famous woman of that era, maybe a few centuries later."

"Bingo. It was in the 15th century and she won some great victories for France."

"Joan of Arc. She became a saint."

"Exactly. But not before having been burned at the stake. I don't see you as a paladin in the 'Richard Boone' sense of the word, although he always made sure that his victims were worthy of the brand of justice he dispensed. What I see that you have in common with Joan of Arc is that you both could be described as naive, and certainly as puppets of the powerful."

After a brief pause, he added, "I'm happy for you in this newfound peace."

They remained quiet for a few moments.

He interrupted the silence with a question, "Do you have something in mind? For the future I mean. Besides the trip to some tropical environ where palm trees sway in the breezes like the hips of the hula girls?"

"Retirement."

"How do you retire from such a career? Isn't that like a CIA agent attempting to retire, or a caporegime for the Genovese family calling it quits?"

"I've got funds stashed away in Geneva and in the Caribbean to maintain my present lifestyle for at least another thirty years. I doubt I'll live that long anyway. I've got multiple identities - not personalities, mind you, identities," and they shared a laugh. Then she continued with little hesitation, "You know I never got a social security number and there's supposed to be enough layers between my clients and me to make it safe. I don't have a clue who pays me and they don't have a clue who does their work for them."

"In theory."

"Right," she sighed, "in theory."

"There's enough doubt, so that you'll plan ahead and take precautions."

"Yes."

"And that's why you wanted to talk to me this morning."

"You're so perceptive!" she said with a warm smile.

Chapter Twenty-four

Thunderstorms in the Smoky Mountains were often spectacular. Terrifying bolts of lightning preceded rafter-shaking thunder that rolled through the valleys. The thunder often echoed for ten seconds or more. Hixon and his K-9 companions were comfortable with the sounds and lightshow. They were not comfortable with an infrequent visitor in their one room log cabin in the mountains. They managed.

"How long you want to be off the radar?" Hixon asked his house guest.

"I've been thinking about that," Thibaut mused. "Have you got a computer? And what's the biggest local paper?"

"I've got a laptop I use for games, but no Internet up here. We could go down into Waynesville and pick up wi-fi in an independent bookstore down there where you can drink coffee and read their newspapers. The big local paper is the Asheville *Citizen-Times*. They might sell the *New York Times* and *The Wall Street Journal* there, too. I'm sure they have wi-fi."

"Do you have an e-mail account? Something I could use without giving away my identity?"

"Did I ever tell you I was in the FBI?" Hixon invoked his government experience. "And I've got a source even better than the Internet."

"I'll bite. Who, what?"

"Mr. Jimmy."

"I bet he's closer, too, isn't he?"

"Yep. It's fine with me if you want to check both. We can stop by his general store on the way to Waynesville."

"He sounds like Sam Drucker."

"Damn. You have got a sense of humor." Hixon was beginning to enjoy the company of this wayfaring stranger.

It was afternoon and neither man had shaved in three days. It would be easy for Hixon to help Thibaut blend in. "When we arrive at Mr. Jimmy's, I'll see if he can fit you a pair of overalls — or maybe some jeans and a camo shirt. People will think you've been hunting with one of those bright orange wind breakers."

"Or that I'm a Tennessee fan," added Thibaut.

Hixon frowned, "I think that's funny, but they got a lot of folks around here that love them Vols, so be careful how you joke about 'em."

Hixon returned to the subject at hand, "It's about a two mile walk straight through the woods and down the mountain to the store. I often leave my truck there in case I need it. Mr. Jimmy don't mind. If we drive from up here, we still got to walk about a mile to reach the Jeep."

"Last week, I would have told you I was in great shape. I'm game, let's walk."

"Good, we can talk all the way. We should be better acquainted."

Thibaut thought to himself, *Oh brother*.

While Hixon was collecting his hiking gear, which included his dogs and his pump shotgun, Thibaut laced up his riding shoes and adjusted his black biking outfit. It was the one set of clothes he had available. A recurring question had been going through his mind, "What the hell happened with the chase vehicles?" Maybe Hixon would know.

When he walked out of the cabin, Hixon was ready. With a wave of his hand, John sent the dogs ahead into the woods.

"They'll clear a trail for us."

"No kidding? How.."

"They scare off the varmints. You know, wolves, coyotes, bears."

"I'll stipulate that you've got the advantage on me here in your environment. Maybe sometime while I'm here, I'll be able to reciprocate."

Hixon replied without commitment, "Well, I've been in your world and prefer this one."

Thibaut hoped he could control the conversation but was also interested in finding out what Hixon knew — and was willing to tell.

"John, what do you know about me?"

"Everybody calls you 'Mr. Thibaut.'"

131

"Good place to start. Please call me either 'Julian' or 'JF'— I have no preference."

"Like Julian Lennon? How 'bout plain 'Jay?'"

"Sure. Fine. Jay it is."

They soon passed the clearing around Hixon's cabin. While Hixon moved with ease through the brush and undergrowth, Thibaut found the going a bit more difficult.

Hixon offered a bit of advice, "Quit watching where you put your foot with every step. After the dogs and me, any snakes would be gone by the time you come along. Watch where you're going, look ahead and all around in the woods. You might miss something interesting."

"Snakes? all right. I'll try. Now, tell what you know about me."

"Well...you got enough money that you can afford private protection. You can afford any kind of transportation you want. And somebody's trying to kill you. They ain't trying too hard, or either they ain't worth a shit. If they'da hired me, you'd be dead by now."

"Are you an assassin?"

"Didn't I tell you that..."

Thibaut cut him off, "Yeah, you told me you worked for the FBI. Go ahead. What else."

"Pointe didn't tell me much. Said he wanted someone available in case they needed some help in the woods. Except he called it the 'wilderness'. Dumb ass. Anyway, I never bothered to go look you up on the Internet, cause..."

Again, Thibaut broke in, "Because you've got Mr. Jimmy. Right?"

"Yep."

"So what did Mr. Jimmy have to say."

What Thibaut heard next stopped him in his tracks. Hixon recounted Thibaut's business history and his spurning of Ole Miss for Vanderbilt. He continued with a more recent synopsis of his business endeavors. It was more accurate than what he had seen about himself on Wikipedia.

"Come on, you're falling behind," Hixon called out. "And

132

don't be surprised at anything Mr. Jimmy comes up with no more."

"I've got to meet this guy," Thibaut remarked.

"You sure will in about an hour. We got some hiking to do."

As they continued their walk through the woods, Thibaut heard Hixon's favorite stories of his times at the FBI, his most harrowing escapades, his brushes with the CIA and as an added bonus, his favorite episodes of *The X Files*, and how he admired the profiling work of 'Bobby' on *Law and Order*. Hixon couldn't resist adding that "the actor who played Bobby was in *Full Metal Jacket*. Remember? He was the one who blew his own brains out in the john after killing the drill instructor."

The more they walked and the more his guide talked, Thibaut couldn't help but wonder if Hixon had managed to blur fact and fiction over the years with each retelling of these stories. After what Thibaut felt like was hours, they reached a clearing and he could see pavement ahead.

"Walking will be a lot easier now. Watch out for these drivers. They use both sides of the road and often straddle the center line."

Then Thibaut asked, "How did you get me from the end of the trail to your cabin? It's quite a walk."

Hixon smiled, "Fireman's carry for a couple a hundred yards. Then, I used a travois."

"That's those things the Indians used isn't it?"

"Yep," confirmed Hixon. "Canadian French term. Fur hunters used two poles connected by a net. Put their cargo on it and drug it with a horse. I didn't have a horse though."

When they walked into "Mr. Jimmy's Grocery" they were greeted with a big smile and a warm "Hello," from behind the counter. For Thibaut, it was like a step back into the early fifties. The wooden floor creaked with every step and a potbellied stove dominated the room. It was the centerpiece around which a pair of wooden rocking chairs and several stools were assembled. All the seating was empty this evening and Mr. Jimmy explained, "Ever'body's either in church, working late, or too drunk to drag

133

their asses down here," and he added a deep baritone laugh.

"Church?" asked Thibaut.

"Misser, this is Winsday, and you jus' showed me you ain't no Baptiss. Least ways not no 'Southern Baptiss.'"

Either Mr. Jimmy had no last name that he wanted to share, or his first name was "Mister." Thibaut shook his hand and had to look down a bit to meet his eyes. He guessed that Jimmy must be about five foot five. He was overweight but moved through the little shop efficiently. The boards were worn from his repetitious trips to and fro helping customers with their orders. His scalp and face were devoid of any hair except for thinning eyebrows and short, almost invisible eye lashes. The top of his head was smooth and easy to see that it had not been shaved — no hair had grown there in years. His mouth and eyes were small and round, like three holes in a bowling ball. His ears stuck out like open car doors. His fingers were short and fat.

When he spoke, he had a lisp that as Chaucer said "made his English sweet upon his tongue." "You been walkin'. Git a Coke over there," and Jimmy pointed to a Coke machine. It was something alien to Thibaut.

There were two reservoirs on the outside, one for money and one for bottle caps. The unit was like a chest model deep freezer but the top wouldn't open until you put your money in. When it did, there appeared a maze through which you had to guide the bottle to an area where it could be lifted from the confines of the machine. The cooler was filled with ten ounce Coca-Colas in the old fashioned sealed glass bottles.

After Thibaut extracted his selection, Hixon spoke up and said, "Now drink it all while we're here, or you have to pay a deposit on the bottle."

"You're kidding, right?" Thibaut asked.

Two silent somber expressions were the unified reply from his host/merchant and guide.

Hixon told Mr. Jimmy, "We need some clothes for my friend here and any news about him if you got any."

Forty-five minutes later, the odd couple was in Hixon's pickup truck heading down highway 74/23 to Waynesville. "We got plenty time, they don't close 'till six o'clock," Hixon said. There was no reply. He looked over and saw that Thibaut's head was back against the seat and he was sound asleep.

Hixon thought to himself, "He must not be in as good a shape as he thought."

Mr. Jimmy had come through in style and Thibaut fit right in. Work boots, camouflage hunting pants, a dark red corduroy long sleeve shirt and a John Deere cap transformed the city man into a good ole country boy. When Hixon parked the truck at Blue Ridge Books, the passenger woke up and rubbed his eyes. They went in and took a seat.

Hixon announced, "I'm having a double latte. What do you want?"

"Coffee, black. I'm going to look around."

Hixon got their drinks and Thibaut headed straight to the newspapers. On the way back to their booth, Hixon noticed a couple of guys at the magazine rack. Were they familiar? Thibaut was busy with the newspapers. By this late hour in the day, they were sold out of everything except yesterday's *Charlotte Observer*. When he returned to the table, Hixon had their coffee and had placed a *Wall Street Journal* in Thibaut's chair.

Hixon answered before the question could be asked, "I found it on another table."

"Let's go. I'm starving."

"I know the place," Hixon confirmed.

A few blocks from the book store, on the way back to Little Canada, Hixon turned into a parking lot that would have accommodated a grocery store. To the left, along the edge of the parking lot were several low buildings. The one in the middle had a neon "OPEN" sign in the front window with each letter flashing in sequence. Outside there were several tables with umbrellas. Hixon approached the hostess and asked for a particular booth. Then he volunteered, "Shirley, we can have a few drinks in the bar if it isn't available." Before they could finish their first drink, they were shown to the last booth along the back wall. The view to the booth from the main dining area was blocked by a half wall around the bus station. Hixon motioned for Thibaut to take the

135

seat facing away from the open dining area and Hixon took the seat against the back wall. Hixon was a self-acknowledged sufferer of what he called the Wild Bill Hickok syndrome — he always sat with his back to the wall. "I learned it when I was in sales," He explained. That was before the FBI. "I would have a prospect in the booth with me and I didn't want someone walking up from behind and interrupt my sales presentation. It was important when I was closing." No one could see Thibaut and he could enjoy a meal in anonymity.

"What's the name of this place?"

Hixon smiled. "It's my favorite restaurant. 'Pasquales' and it's not part of a chain. I eat here often. The chicken marsala is fantastic. So is the filet mignon."

They both decided on the steak and topped it off with strawberry/champagne soup. Hixon said it was a "house special" and he preferred it for desert.

Hixon expected his new friend to sleep all the way back now that he had eaten, but Thibaut wanted to talk.

"The idea of staying below the radar is appealing — at least until this meeting I'm scheduled to attend in Atlanta. It's important. And, it's on Friday."

"That's day after tomorrow."

"Yes."

"You claimed you could make me appear there. You ready to make good on that? Money is no object."

"Really?"

"Really."

"Here's what I've got in mind."

136

Part Six

Claudia had been unable to return to Baton Rouge in time for Dr. Thibaut's funeral, but when she did, she went straight to see Miss Lil. The Thibaut home was still her domain at the time of the visit and it would be months before the estate was settled. The icon of Stanford Drive would remain secure for a while. They embraced at the door and Miss Lil showed her into Dr. Thibaut's favorite room — his library. It was a large room made cozy by the bookcases that lined the walls. The bookcases were above cabinets that surrounded the room and all the woodwork was painted a brilliant glossy white. The good doctor's desk backed by a credenza dominated the end of the rectangular shaped room opposite an entrance that featured French doors. Rather than chairs for his guests, there was an oversized antique couch covered in red crushed velvet that faced the desk. Two small matching coffee tables separated the desk and the couch and each featured a glass top. Beneath the glass was a collection of photographs, theatre tickets and printed formal invitations that documented family history for decades. Of course, they sat on the couch and Miss Lil brought in a pot of fresh brewed Community Dark Roast coffee.

"You remember what I told you about sunsets, don't you?" Lilly had asked.

"Yes, ma'am, I do. I'll never forget it," Claudia replied.

"Well, Dr. Thibaut's passing was one with a beautiful clear sunset. No clouds to be seen, but a beautiful afterglow." Lillie put her coffee cup on the table, raised her glasses and wiped her eyes with the ever-present white lace handkerchief.

Claudia thought a moment and at the risk of sounding like a challenge, pressed ahead with her question, "Do you think that people can have a cloudy life — one that would have beautiful clouds at sunset, but, aaah, still have had troubles?"

"Honey, no life goes by without problems. We all have our clouds. Remember that man in Lil' Abner?" They shared a laugh and Lilly continued, "I'm sure Dr. Thibaut had his concerns, but they would have been those wispy little clouds that the wind carries away with ease. Sure wouldn't have been

137

anything like a mushroom cloud!" She winked at Claudia,
reached out, and hugged her tight.

Chapter Twenty-five

Julian Thibaut and his group had begun their motorcycle tour of the Dragon's Tail. The constant low rumble of the Harleys mixed with the chainsaw whine of the sport bikes combined to produce enough decibels that it was hard for Gerald Pointe to hear on his headset. He was disappointed. Even with the noise reduction feature, there was too much background sound. He could make out conversation, but most other sounds were obliterated. It was no wonder that he did not hear the sound of Sweeney's bike exploding.

In less than a half hour on the road, they had driven into an ambush. Now they had been in a shootout for almost five minutes. It felt like five hours.

Pointe shouted into his mic, "Fire."

Webster, in the chase group, about a quarter mile behind and on a stretch of road overlooking the shootout, replied, "Copy that. Be there in a second."

The first SUV arrived in less than a minute and was parked between the bikes and the wooded area where the shots had originated. The shooting stopped.

Pointe and Gregg were still crouched behind their bikes. Several empty .45-caliber magazines were strewn about on the pavement along with more than a dozen spent shotgun cartridges.

Gregg and another member of the Thibaut team were gearing up to go after the ambushers and Pointe stopped them.

"Let's cut our losses here. Probably wouldn't find them anyway." They put the pieces of Sweeney's bike into the back of the SUVs and wrapped his body in a tarp.

Gregg handed his cell phone to Pointe, "It's Chuck Martin at the airport in Knoxville."

Pointe took the phone, "Chuck, what's the flying time to Bryson City in your Huey?"

Pointe listened then replied, "Yes, I know they have an airport there — but I don't want to use it. We've got an extraction. One dead, one wounded. We have an EMT with us. Call me when you're over Bryson City and I'll have you a landing spot located. Go."

"Delta Echo 2, out," answered Martin.

It was then that Gregg noticed the blood. Pointe had been hit in the left shoulder.

"Mr. Pointe, you've been hit."

"Yes. Can't raise my left arm. Happened when I went to help our mountain man with the boss."

"Yeah I was wondering about that. How come none of our team is with them?"

"Trust me on that one. Where's Webster?"

The EMT had been driving the lead SUV and didn't know he was needed until Gregg noticed the blood. Gregg waved him over and he started pulling back Pointe's riding gear to examine the wound.

"No exit hole in the jacket. Where does it hurt? Shoulder?"

Pointe still showed no pain. "Let's get the hell outta here. You can look at it all you want in the truck. We've got to make it to Bryson City in forty-five minutes."

Within five minutes, the convoy of two SUVs and the operable bikes were on the road. Gerald Pointe was pleased with the efficiency of his team.

Webster had Pointe stripped to the waist and could see the wound better. "Doesn't look like it hit an artery. The blood's dark, indicating damage to veins. There's a pretty big artery in your arm that goes up under the trapezius muscle. If it had been hit, there would be bright red blood all over the place. So you're lucky there. Pain on a one to ten?"

"I have a high tolerance for pain."

"Pain on a one to ten, please."

"OK, three or four. I know it's there."

"What if you raise your arm?"

"I can't."

"Must have hit some muscle tissue. Since there's no exit wound, it must not have penetrated the shoulder blade. You may be lucky if you don't have any broken bones."

"What's the prognosis?"

140

"Excellent, barring any complications. I'm going to start an IV. You need fluids and we need a line open for drugs. We don't want you to go into shock. You'll need an antibiotic pretty soon for sure. You allergic to anything?"

"No. Do your job, I need to talk to Gregg."

Pointe had declined Gregg's offer to ride out ahead of the SUVs and chosen another. He was beginning to trust Gregg and appreciated his sense of loyalty — both to him and Thibaut. Instead, he had put Gregg in the truck with himself. If he passed out, he wanted Gregg to take over.

"OK, Mr. Gregg, you may have a battlefield promotion here, if I pass out. Call Rosemary. See if she's heard from the boss. Make sure she has your cell phone number and that it works. I've got to keep mine. After we meet the helicopter, you take Fanceca and go to Waynesville. That's convenient to both Asheville and Hixon's place up in the mountains near Tuckaseegee. Don't worry about Hixon. Former FBI. He's got a network like you wouldn't believe and enough influence to have whatever he wants — even in retirement. Keep a low profile and stay in touch. If the boss calls in, you need to move fast. Unless he asks for help, stay in the background. Keep the bikes maintained. There are several places around Waynesville and Maggie Valley that cater to bikers. You can buy some clothes and whatever you need. Put it on expense."

Gregg was taking it all in, "What's the timeframe?"

"Thibaut is supposed to be at a big meeting in Atlanta on Friday. If he's OK, he'll show up there. We need to be there, too — details later."

Gregg felt his phone vibrate, "Call comin' in."

He answered and said, "Yeah?" then listened a moment.

Fanceca was driving, "Fan. How far are we from Bryson City? Martin says his ETA is about fifteen."

Fanceca took a quick look at the GPS and said, "Damn. He's way ahead of us. He's making great time."

"all right. Stand by, Chuck."

Pointe and Gregg looked at the map and checked the GPS and came up with a plan.

141

"Listen up, Fan. I'm giving Martin the new rendezvous. Meet us about a mile east of the junction of Highway 28 and Sweetwater Road. There should be plenty of clear space to set down right across from the Stecoah Diner."

"I see where Stecoah Road hits 28 and an open field right there. Got it," Martin replied.

Gregg turned to Pointe who appeared drained. His face was beginning to pale a bit, "Martin's bird got enough room?"

Pointe perked up, smiled and showed some enthusiasm with his reply, "You'll love this. I hope I'm awake to see it."

Pointe turned to Webster and asked, "Did you spike that IV with something to knock me out? I'm starting to fade."

The EMT smiled and said, "Why do think you're still feeling   no   pain?"
Pointe leaned his head back on the head rest and spoke up toward the ceiling, "That helicopter is Martin's hobby. He bought a Vietnam-era Huey. Tons of money and lots of time restoring it. Keeps it in top flying shape. Not many left anymore and none in this good a shape. Every time he shows up in it, I expect to hear Wagner. He may even be in uniform. You ever heard of the CAF?"

Gregg noticed that Pointe slurred the initials of the Confederate Air Force as his head turned a bit to the side then his neck muscles relaxed. He was out. Gregg looked at Webster. The EMT gave him a thumbs-up and said, "He's stable. When he wakes up, we should be in Knoxville. With our connections, he'll receive the best care available and never see the inside of a hospital."

Within a half hour, Martin had lifted off with Webster, Pointe, and Sweeney's body on board en route to Knoxville. Gregg and Fanceca got two of the remaining Harleys and separated from the rest of the group. They enjoyed the ride into Waynesville and spent an hour or so riding around studying the lay of the land. By nightfall, they had a room at the Oak Park Inn on South Main Street. A tavern within walking distance looked appealing and the man at the front desk recommended it.

"Where you'ins from?" the server asked as she brought

them menus. She was about five foot five and full figured. Not fat, but maybe twenty pounds more than necessary. When the subject came up with her friends, she said, "I'm a few inches too short," and would laugh. Both colors of her hair, jet black and fire engine red came from bottles. Her piercings and tattoos made her a walking billboard for the local parlor.

They looked at each other questioning her greeting. It was alien to both of them.

Fanceca, from the deep South tried first, "We-uns are from Mississippi."

She gave them a quizzical look and replied, "Sounds like you ain't from the mountains. What y'all want to drink?"

Gregg smiled, "I'm from Texas and 'y'all' is a lot more familiar to me. What do you have on draft?"

They ordered and with each visit to their table, she got more familiar. Her name tag read "Veronica" but she said, "You can call me Ronnie."

Ronnie proved to be a valuable source of information about the area. She directed them to two gun shops for ammo, a nearby Harley dealer, and the town's Walmart for "anything you want — that Wallyworld carries. If they don't have what you want, you're screwed. You-ins might find jus' what you want somewheres else, but it'll cost ya' an arm and a leg."

They left a generous cash tip and as they were leaving, Gregg asked, "Where can we find the morning papers tomorrow?"

Ronnie didn't hesitate. Her body language screamed, "I'll come to your room, tell me where you're staying, please." She pointed back up the street toward their motel and said, "In that little strip shopping center by the Oak Park Inn. It's a place called Blue Ridge Books."

143

Chapter Twenty-six

The dinner for the ITTA Group was about to conclude in the private dining room of London's Reform Club. "I hope everyone enjoyed the day, the meetings, and tonight's dinner." Farrell said as he was about to dismiss the group. He turned to Gore and said with a big smile, "Martha, thank you for the dance." Everyone chuckled. "I'm off to a meeting in Atlanta and a few weeks in the States. If you need anything, you all know how to reach Star. Good evening."

Everyone stood in unison and Farrell worked his way around the room with personal goodbyes for each. To his delight, no one wanted a last minute one-on-one. He stepped out of the private dining room and found his bodyguard waiting.

"The car's ready, sir. Waiting downstairs."

"Thanks. Any word from Star?"

"Yes, sir. She's back at the apartment."

Farrell kept an apartment in London. Even though his company was headquartered there, he spent most of his time elsewhere, often in Switzerland or the States. In spite of the fact that his personal wealth afforded him the availability of any vice and pleasure he desired, he had managed to keep his desires limited to sex and either Chivas Regal or Wild Turkey.

Since the AIDS scare of the 80s he had been careful with his liaisons. After hiring Star Braun in the early 90s he had been with no one else. He suspected she had not been as careful. In spite of her possible infidelities, she and one other had earned Farrell's trust. The other was Warren Byrd.

Warren was like a father to him and he often confided in him. It was hard to find someone with whom he could reveal his innermost secrets — and even Warren Byrd did not know them all. Farrell trusted Byrd. He trusted him more than any other and never felt like he had made a mistake with that trust. Byrd was reliable and over the years had often made decisions that were best for the company even when they were not best for Byrd.

He picked up his cell phone and hit the memory button for Star.

144

"I'm waiting on you."

"I'll be there in a few. In the limo now."

"Was about to blow dry my hair."

"Don't. I want you drenched."

They had been together for twenty years and he still was able to make her heart pound. This was a first. She slipped out of the thick white terry cloth robe and let it drop to the floor.

"Call me when you're in the building. But I won't answer it. I'm getting back into the shower."

"You got it."

Their timing was spot on. Farrell dismissed his guard for the night. He used them while abroad and when in public. Never needed one in the States.

He opened the door and tossed his suit coat onto a chair. As he began to loosen his tie he saw Star enter from a cloud of steam pouring out of the bath. She was wearing nothing but beads of hot water, glistening as they rolled down her face, arms, and chest.

Stepping into the room with cooler air gave her goose bumps. Her hair was soaked and pulled back into a wet ponytail that fell well past her shoulders and supplied a constant stream of water down her back. Wet, her blonde hair appeared darker. The water streaming off her nude body created a soggy trail across the carpet. When they were near enough for him to reach her, she stopped and surrendered by allowing her arms to fall at her sides. With one hand, he took the wet ponytail and pulled her head back. She looked up and saw him lean in. She shut her eyes and gently parted her lips for the kiss.

Later, Farrell awoke and realized he was alone on the carpet. She noticed and called out, "I'll be right back with some wine."

While she was at the bar, he moved to the sofa and stretched out to relax. It had been a long day and he was enjoying himself now. He could tell that Star was as well. While she was serving the wine she lowered the lights and opened the drapes onto the balcony. The half moon and city lights of London, many floors below, added a romantic appeal to the room. They had the wine and each other again.

"Should I open another bottle of wine?"

Farrell smiled and whispered, "Do you want more wine or breakfast? It's after two. When is our flight?"

"It's whenever you say it is," she giggled.

Then she continued, "We're flying from Heathrow to Hartsfield. I allowed a day for travel and then we're due at the meeting at 6:00 p.m. Friday."

"I'll need a shower, too. So what did you find out while I was having dinner."

"Challenger's connections to the council are confirmed. Remember last week we discussed his experience with Skull and Bones?"

Farrell nodded.

"Well several of his 'fraternity' brothers are in now and it turns out that our boy, Griffin was a damned legacy himself. Both his father and grandfather were in."

"Bastard's been holding out on me. I damned well should have hit him with a baseball bat."

"Yes, and there's more. He's going to try to leverage his influence with the council with you."

"So..."

"He's going to make a play for Nigel's position."

"Smart move, but he hasn't proven himself with his own division."

"That's why he feels like he needs leverage."

"This accounts for what happened during cocktails before the meeting tonight."

"Griffin approached Nigel and threatened him?"

"Close. Maybe. Warren and I were watching them from across the room and something Challenger said got the old boy upset. We could see the reaction from across the room."

"What else?"

"Martha better hope those researchers of hers win the Nobel. We're going to be attacked with some big suits over the diabetes thing."

Farrell was growing weary from the long day of meetings,

146

sex, and alcohol. He was in no mood for bad news. He leaned back on the sofa. Star responded by leaning in against him. She knew he liked to feel her naked body against his, no matter what the topic of conversation.

"Well, we know the Nobel can be fixed."

"Helping put in the fix four years ago didn't end up benefiting us now did it?"

"The one for the global warming thing did help, even if it ended in 'Climategate'."

"Let's give that to Frank before it explodes."

"He's already on it. That's why he didn't attend the meeting or the dinner today."

"I figured as much."

"Anything else before we rest?"

"Got a late update from the team in Tennessee. Thibaut is still alive but whereabouts unknown. Our mole was some security guy named Sweeney. He's dead. The idiot hit team blew him up."

"How'd that happen?"

"I don't know if it was Gerald Pointe's idea or someone else's, but they had five or six riders all dressed alike. All about the same height and build. Even had identical helmets. Sounds like our guys got anxious and hit the first bike."

"Shit. I should have hired Pointe when I had the chance."

"There was a big shootout and Thibaut escaped. Sounds like some passerby dragged him into the woods. Then they disappeared. The field report says Thibaut was hit. Not sure how bad he was hurt."

"Gotta eliminate that guy. Plan B?"

"Other arrangements with some shooter with a solid reputation. Cost a bundle."

"Doesn't matter. When's the hit?"

"There may be some excitement before the meeting in Atlanta."

She stood up, took his wine glass and set it on the end table with hers. Then while standing in front of him, she leaned forward placing each hand on the back of the sofa near his shoulders and buried his face in her cleavage.

147

Then she whispered, "Once more darling..."

Chapter Twenty-seven

Hixon's dogs ran out to meet his pickup truck as he backed into his favorite parking spot next to the deuce and a half. It was facing the road.

"I like to be headed out when I'm ready to leave," he explained to Jay. "It's almost ten o'clock and we need to leave by five in the morning to take care of everything."

Thibaut asked, "How long did you say to Atlanta?"

"About three hours. But we aren't going all the way in tomorrow are we?"

"Nope. We both need some new clothes for the meeting. Are you hard to fit?"

"I don't think so. Why do you ask?"

"Well, can you go into a fine men's store and find a suit off the rack and have it fit you without a lot of tailoring? Damn, Hixon. What did you wear when you worked for the FBI?"

"Custom-made suits. Don't worry about clothes, I got that taken care of. When we reach an area where I have cell phone reception, one call will fix it."

"Tell me more. Although I'm sure you will anyway," Thibaut grumbled through a smile.

"An old buddy of mine has a shop in Roswell, a suburb of Atlanta. Guess what the name of his shop is."

"Area 51."

"You got it. It's hidden way in the back of another store. He's an old hippie dude and lives in another suburb called Woodstock."

"And his name is Yasgur, right?"

"Good try. Close, but no cigar. I'll give you one more guess."

"Neil Young?"

"Another good guess. But wrong. It's Robert Dillon, as in Matt. Goes by the nickname, "Bobby.""

"Does your bullshit ever end?" Thibaut enquired.

"Naw, and I'm just gettin' warmed up. Before I kick into second gear with my stories, tell me more about this meeting

149

we're going to. I'll be armed."

"They have metal detectors you'll have to pass through."

"This ought to do the trick." Hixon reached into his pocket and produced a current FBI identification card and badge.

"Thought you said you were retired."

"I am."

"This is current. Is it real? I mean, valid?" Thibaut was perplexed.

"It's not important for you to know that. What's important is that it'll help me arrive at where I want to go. If it don't, I got one from the CIA, too. Screw their metal detectors. What are the chances anyone else there will bring their own personal FBI agent with them?"

"None. Quite a few of them will have their own security though. Once we go into the meeting room, you'll have to stay outside with the other non-members."

"Tell me more."

"There are several meetings and a reception. That's what starts the activity. It'll be in a large meeting room at a place in Atlanta called 'The Buckhead Club.' Ever heard of it?"

"No."

"The opening reception always reminds me of a fraternity 'smoker.' Current members hobnobbing with each other and prospective members."

"Prospective members?"

"Yes. This is an exclusive organization and it isn't easy to become a member. Once in, seats on the board are coveted — and hard to attain."

"It seems logical, that you wouldn't be able to tell me what y'all meet about, but can you tell me the purpose of this exclusive club?"

"Hmmm...well. OK, ever heard of Jekyll Island?"

"Oh shit. Don't tell me all the conspiracy theories are true."

"Try this analogy. Suppose you have a huge multi-national corporation. Doesn't matter the name or which one. And you've got thousands, maybe millions of stockholders. You with me?"

"I can guess where you're going. The top ten or twelve stock holders meet and it doesn't matter if they're on the board of directors or not. The big money people pull the strings."

"You're warm. They would have significant investments if they're in the top one percent of stock holders."

"The one percenters."

Thibaut nodded, "Yes, and these people talk about what they think would be best for the company — and of course their return on investment."

Hixon picked up the ball and began to run, "So, if what they decide they want the company to do, actually happens..."

Thibaut continued, "Was it the result of a conspiracy? Or was it the result of informed business decisions based on the best — and I do mean the best — information available?"

Hixon began to show Thibaut that he was well read. "I'm familiar with FDR's famous quote, except he was talking about politics, not publicly held companies."

"You mean his quote about what happens in politics is not by chance?"

"You got it," Hixon confirmed, and then continued, "I remember stories, maybe urban legends, maybe historical fact, about several families with names like Browning, Colt, Winchester, Remington, Smith, Wesson, all staying on Jekyll Island for a big meeting. Somehow, the stories connect these folks to the U.S. involvement in the First World War."

Thibaut smiled and said, "You're about to scratch the surface. But that's not our group."

"Yeah, right. There's all kinds of groups, from the Masons and Shriners to the Bilderbergers to the Knights Templar and the Illuminati and the AFL-CIO. I remember when Jimmy Carter was President the press made a big deal out of him joining the Trilateral Commission and how much influence the Council on Foreign Relations had — or didn't have. What's their magazine called?"

Thibaut smiled again and answered, "*Foreign Affairs.*"

"Oh, all right, I was thinking *The New Republic*, but

anyway, back to your analogy. Your group, whoever or whatever they call themselves represents a few of the one per centers — or more like the upper one percent of the one percent — and y'all like to have some influence in world affairs. 'Deep Throat' was right. 'Follow the money.'"

"We're to a point now where I can't comment or react to much of what you say. Let's talk about our arrangement and what I'm paying you to do."

Hixon shuffled around in his seat and got comfortable behind the wheel again. "We're about to cross the border into Georgia now and it's almost sunrise. You hungry?"

"Starving."

"When was the last time you ate in a Waffle House?"

"Not since Vanderbilt."

Their waitress had a name badge that read, "Betty Lou" and the moment she asked what they wanted, Thibaut responded with, "The All Star breakfast. Over easy. Grits. Toast and bacon. And I want the waffle really brown."

She turned to Hixon and he said, "I'll have the same, except add a T-bone, medium." Then he turned to Thibaut and said, "You remembered pretty well over the years. How about scattered, smothered, and covered?"

"I prefer scattered and smothered, well done."

While they were drinking their coffee waiting on their orders to arrive, Hixon called his hippie friend, Robert Dillon. "Bobby, it's John Hixon. What you doing?"

"I'm on the pavement thinking 'bout the government."

Dillon shouted into the phone like some people do when they think it's required because of long distances. Hixon held the phone away from his ear due to the volume and Thibaut could hear the conversation with ease.

"I'll be in Roswell in a couple hours with a friend. We need some business clothes. You know, suits."

"He says, 'Sing while you slave' and I just get bored."

"Yeah, right. You have my measurements. They haven't changed. My buddy here looks like about a 42 Long."

Hixon looked at Thibaut and said, "That about right,

152

Jay?"

Thibaut nodded and asked out loud, "Does he always use lyrics for conversation?"

Hixon smiled and said to Thibaut, "You don't have to sit and wonder why, babe. If'n you don't know by now," and they both laughed.

Then back into the phone, Hixon asked, "So how's Sweet Melinda?"

Dillon shouted, "The peasants call her the goddess of gloom."

"Give her my love and tell her that the last time we were together, she left me howling at the moon."

Thibaut could hear a deep raspy cough come from the phone. It sounded like the last gasp of a dying soul with chronic lung disease.

Hixon was about to end the conversation; he could see Betty Lou coming toward them with her arms loaded with plates and saucers balancing their breakfast better than the guy on Ed Sullivan spinning plates. "So you think you can fix us up?"

"Yes, I think it can be easily done. Out on Highway sixty-one," and Dillon disconnected.

The two travelers laughed and attacked their breakfast with little conversation. Betty Lou brought them a copy of the *Atlanta Journal Constitution* and Thibaut scanned it while eating. He looked up at Hixon and asked, "Would you like a section of the paper?"

"Nope. I don't read 'em anymore. I guess that's why I didn't know anything about you before Mr. Jimmy gave me his report."

"I grew up in Mississippi, graduated from Vanderbilt and you've figured out my financial situation. I've got offices in New York and Baltimore."

Hixon was interested in his new friend now, "Family?"

"Never married. No siblings. Mom died long ago and my father died several years ago. He was a professor at LSU."

"Hmmm. What did he teach?" Hixon sensed that Thibaut was warming to the topic. His demeanor and body language

153

suggested strong ties to his late father.

"He started out teaching English composition to law students and pre-med students. In his later years he became the chairman of several committees for students working on advanced degrees. You know, master and doctoral candidates."

"Did you see him often?"

"Not as much as I'd like to have. You know the old thing about careers creating obstacles. Are you a fan of Nilsson?"

"Schmilsson," Hixon replied with a wide smile. They were on the same wave length — thinking about the same song.

Thibaut continued. "But I did manage to call him every week."

After a long pause he sighed, "We had some great conversations."

Hixon decided to press on hoping for some insight, "Y'all talk about anything other than the usual father/son stuff?"

"He was private and protective of his students, but managed to tell me some great stories about them while protecting their identities."

"Such as."

"Some of the last few conversations we had involved this dude — well, I never found out if the candidate was male or female. Doesn't matter I guess. Anyway, this was a master's candidate and Dad was enthralled with the course of study, the theme of the thesis, and the research."

"What was it?"

"Group dynamics. He even recruited me. I've got some contacts in the entertainment industry and this guy wanted to meet some of the more original artists that worked with illusions, so I got them connected. Once, Dad told me that this person was a master of disguise and could disappear right in front of you."

"How did your father die?"

"He had fought diabetes for years. He watched his diet and was compliant with his meds."

"Then...."

"The drug that was helping him the most was experimental. He was involved in some trials for a new drug

154

application. The company developing it was bought out and the new owners killed the funding for the research. His doctors found it difficult to keep his blood sugar regulated without the benefit of the new drug and within six months, he was dead."

"Sorry to hear. There must be more to the story."

"Maybe, but not now," replied Thibaut.

"Why would anyone want to kill you?"

"I've got some ideas, but I can't share any of them with you."

"But you're convinced that you have a traitor on board?"

"Or a mole for the opposition."

"It ain't Pointe?"

"That's one thing I'm sure of, but nevertheless, Pointe hired someone that he should not have."

"When are you going to let your folks know that you'll make the meeting?"

"They're already in Atlanta. The plan is that unless they have some confirmation that I'm dead, they won't report me as missing, and they'll be in Atlanta ready for us."

Hixon was shifting into another mode, "Tell me about the people in the inner circle. The ones you'll be with behind closed doors while I'm waiting outside. Do you have any concern that one or more of them would attack you in the secret meeting?"

"No. I'm one of, if not the youngest. Most of these guys are old geezers that I could knock out with one punch. They're too smart to try anything in Atlanta if any of them are after me. They wouldn't dream of killing me anyway. They'd arrange to kill my interests."

"Will the reception have a lot of guests? You mentioned pledges?" Hixon went back to the fraternity analogy.

Thibaut smiled, "There will be lots of guests at the reception. Two or three times the number of members on the council. Men and women. You'll see some stunning women. Many are there as distractions. Some are available if you're interested."

"I'm kinda in a relationship."

"If I guessed that it was an older woman, would I be

155

right?"

"None of your business. Quid pro quo. When you're more forthcoming about your club."

"Fair enough."

"I would usually arrive in a limo. This time we'll slip into the building without attracting attention. I'd like to arrive at the reception with no fanfare or advance notice. Maybe we can pick up some clues by the reactions of people when we work the crowd. I'll introduce you as an associate. Pointe has been with me several times and everyone knows he's my security man. Perhaps with him not there, they may think my guard is down. Can you pull off this charade?"

Hixon replied with firm confidence, "I won an Academy Award once. Don't worry about me. I'll be in character and deliver on my promise. You'll come home alive."

They paid on the way to Hixon's truck and got back on the road. The sun was up now and above the mountains.

"Let's go. Lot's to do today," Hixon said.

Chapter Twenty-eight

Claudia Barry felt her cell phone vibrate. The text message read, "stag."

So, she thought to herself. *It's The Buckhead Club. Glad I made reservations when I did.*

She had made reservations several weeks before when she was notified of the final two choices for the meeting. Now she would contact the three hotels that were out of the picture, cancel the reservations there and destroy the cell phone that had received the text.

The Intercontinental Buckhead Hotel was one of her favorite places to stay in Atlanta.

She knew the concierge, Jacques. He was a brilliant man who spoke five languages, that she knew about. He had helped her many times and she was always generous with tips.

Several years ago, she had succeeded in deceiving him with one of her disguises and considered that a significant benchmark. If she could pull the wool over Jacques's eyes, she could fool anybody.

Jacques knew her as Miss Evelyn. Evelyn DeVille from New Orleans was one of Claudia's most effective aliases. Miss DeVille was in her mid-seventies. She had blue hair, red fingernails and wore "Harry Caray" style eyeglasses. Her voice cracked and wavered from falsetto to a midrange alto. Miss DeVille had long suffered from osteoporosis and seemed to enjoy telling everyone who would listen about her condition. Observers who were prone to stereotyping and profiling would have deduced as much from the defining hump in her back and stoop-shouldered posture. One of her shoes was built up to adjust for her short leg syndrome, another favorite topic of conversation which made listeners even more uncomfortable and eager to either change the subject or find another person with whom to chat. When excited, the shiny chrome quad cane became like an orchestra conductor's baton. It was also a great pointing tool for directions. She checked into a room at the Intercontinental and requested a room on the side of the property facing North.

Several pieces of her equipment had arrived the day before by FedEx. The barrel of her rifle was concealed in her walking cane.

The last few days in Florida had been busy and focused.

Journal entry:

Tuesday

"Went to Walmart and purchased a barber's trimmer kit. Didn't want to go to a salon. Too easy to do it myself. Got some black hair dye from CVS. Cut my hair down to about two inches and then dyed it solid black. Sent the cut hair to my wig maker. Be nice to have a natural wig of my own hair. Could come in handy. Tomorrow, I'll cut it down to a half inch — no bangs. The wigs and wardrobe should arrive a day before me. Began closing and locking the day-tight compartments last week. Started in earnest today. By tomorrow, I'll be in total focus and have the past and the future locked away in their own compartments: Hixon, painting, sunsets, crying, Debert, Dr. Thibaut, Miss Lil, the islands, the third man, retirement, all of it — including the persistent Mr. Debert's doors with question marks on them. I'll be ready to do what I do so well unencumbered by other thoughts."

Another guest registered at the Intercontinental the day after Miss DeVille arrived. It was a youngish male punker who was openly gay. Joey "Randy" Randle wore all black leather, black fingernail polish, and black lipstick. He managed to acquire a room on the north end of the property. His room was on a lower floor and faced The Buckhead Club. As soon as Randy entered the room, he placed the "Do Not Disturb" sign on the door. It would remain in place throughout the duration of his stay. Within an hour of arriving, he called the front desk and asked if either or both of the adjoining rooms were available for friends arriving the next day. They were, or would be, so he reserved them both — for "friends". The first night of his stay, he ordered dinner from room service, made a pass at the male server, and left a memorable tip.

Claudia Barry was pleased that each of her incarnations had passed the "Jacques test" with ease. The venerable concierge had been sympathetic towards Miss DeVille and professional in his polite response to Randy. Jacques was also pleased to have been finished with each of their interactions when done. Now that each character had made their entrance and established themselves on stage, either or both could host guests of a variety of sexes and appearances. No one at the hotel would see Claudia Barry during the stays of her alter egos.

At 2:00 p.m. on the Friday afternoon of Farrell's meeting at the Buckhead Club, Randy Randle would have a visitor. A middle aged man with short black hair dressed in a dark, three piece business suit would come calling. After his arrival, no one at the Intercontinental Hotel would see either him, or Randy Randle again. Later, that same Friday, one of Randy's female friends would leave. In the event that she would be seen, witnesses would report that she had long auburn hair, black fishnet stockings and black Chuck Taylor sneakers. She would be wearing a ripped "guinea-T" that made her bra-less cleavage a focal point and a skirt that was two or three inches too short. Between the legs and the chest, no one would remember any details of her face or care about what she was carrying.

Randy's friend would use a stairwell rather than the elevator to make her exit and she, too, would never be seen again.

Three final exit plans were available, unless there was an emergency situation in which she had to be creative.

The first choice would be for Miss DeVille to check out Friday evening with all her luggage in tow and take a taxi to a strip mall in Marietta.

Second choice would be to leave dressed as an off duty member of the housekeeping staff. It had been easy enough to acquire a uniform that fit.

Third choice would feature a middle-aged jogger on Peachtree Road who would turn on Highland Drive and then hail a cab. It would be disappointing to leave all her gear behind, but if she did retire, she wouldn't need it anyway. Randy's room was scheduled to be occupied for several more days anyway. She hoped that if any of her gear was left there, it would be a day or two before it was discovered. Over the years, the shooter had been required to improvise before, abandon gear before, and it had never been a problem. Before.

Friday night, she would stay over with Hixon's friend, Mr. Dillon, the hippie haberdasher, masquerading as his fictitious wife, "Sweet Melinda."

Chapter Twenty-nine

Gerald Pointe and his team had rooms in Atlanta at the Savannah Suites on Peachtree Road near the end of the runways of the DeKalb-Peachtree Airport. It was Friday morning and he called the corporate office in Baltimore for an update.

"Nothing. No word yet," Rosemary Woods was as emotionless as a police dispatcher sending a unit on a routine call. In all her years of service with Julian Thibaut, she had been through a lot and had learned to expect anything and be surprised by nothing.

Gerald Pointe conserved his words over the cell phone call as well, "Same here. We're in position. Gregg and I will be at the club. Fanceca is at the apartment. The two SUVs will be close, one near each location. Martin has the Gulfstream at DeKalb-Peachtree. He can be ready to take off on short notice."

"Thanks. We'll be in touch."

He snapped shut the cell phone and turned to Gregg, "Since we haven't heard anything, other than your sighting in Waynesville, I'm sure the boss will show up at the meeting. I've been to these meetings with him before and I'm sure some of the people here will recognize me. They won't remember my name, but they'll associate my face with Thibaut. When they see his security team here, they'll back off of any attempts. When he sees us, he should feel better knowing we're here. Remember now, let him approach us. We don't know what's on his mind or how he wants to play this. You got me?"

"Yes, sir." Gregg was looking forward to this opportunity. He was pleased with his performance at the Dragon's Tail shootout and eager to follow it up with a show of consistency. He was excited and confident. He was comfortable in his business suit and the communications gear. The earpiece was almost invisible and the mike on his lapel eliminated the need to talk into his wrist. He didn't want to look like a Secret Service agent.

Pointe went back over the incident at the bookstore, "You say you're certain it was him?"

Gregg answered with confidence, "I recognized Hixon

161

first."

Fanceca nodded in agreement, "The boss was dressed in camo and needed a shave. I never seen him that casual before. It was hard to make out that it was him."

Gregg picked up the narrative, "We didn't approach them. The boss never looked our way, but Hixon did."

"And no reaction?" Pointe asked again to confirm.

"No sir." Gregg and Fanceca answered in unison.

Pointe turned to Ben Webster, the third man in the group that would enter the club. "You'll be the only one of us that's armed, at first. And you've got the case with the weapons for Gregg and me."

Webster was attentive even though they'd gone over the plan several times. He would go in as far as possible until they reached the metal detector and internal security. In addition to the Uzi and ammo inside the case, Webster would be carrying enough for the three of them with easier access. He would have shoulder holsters on each side, two sidearms and a third on his belt in the back. With one ankle holster, he would have six pistols available at a moment's notice.

Pointe's shoulder was sore. It had caused him more trouble with time. Torn muscle tissue, cartilage, and the bruise turned out to be more painful than the initial wound itself. He couldn't use it much, but tomorrow, in a suit, it would appear natural at his side and attract no attention. Gregg and Fanceca had stayed in Waynesville until late Thursday afternoon and neither seen nor heard anything about the shooting. Thursday morning they had gorged on a monster breakfast at Clyde's Restaurant. The man at the front desk at their motel had said it was where the locals eat and they were able to sit in a booth next to three sheriff's deputies. Fanceca had struck up a conversation with them and asked about the Dragon's Tail. All three men were familiar with it and none volunteered any current news, so Fanceca pressed with a question.

"We're thinking about riding the Tail this weekend. Other than traffic, is it safe?"

None of the deputies knew of anything to report and one

162

said he was a bike rider and had enjoyed his trip up there.

So, Fanceca tried again, "Last night at Bogart's, we heard some people at the next table talking about a shoot-out involving some bikers. Where was that?"

Again, none of the deputies had any news. They came across as believable when they said they were uninformed of any violence or shootings. With nothing to report, the two had contacted Pointe and received their instructions to ride into Atlanta Thursday night. Pointe and Chuck Martin met them at the hotel.

Pointe had given them the overall plan, "Chuck, we may need to get out of Atlanta fast. When we arrive at the club, we'll call you and you do your preflight checklist and file a flight plan for takeoff within an hour. You can always adjust it for a later time if necessary, but we don't know what we're walking into. Fan, if there's no activity at the apartment, let me know and I'll decide on what I want you to do. May need you to meet us en route or be available to cut off anyone that may be tailing us. OK?"

"Got it."

"Here's what I'm thinking. One scenario is that everything is and will be all right. The boss and our mountain man, Hixon, will show up at the meeting. Hixon is former FBI. I'm thinking the boss will have him there as his bodyguard. Nobody makes a move on Thibaut at the meeting, and afterwards, we reconnect and bring him home."

He looked at the pilot, Martin, and said, "In that case, we may not be able to leave until late Friday night or maybe Saturday morning."

"I'm expecting that the boss will be there and we can make contact with him on his way into the reception. I don't care if we do nothing but make eye contact, we can let him know we're there. He can decide if he wants us in the reception. My other scenario is not as optimistic, but that's what he pays me for. That's why Webster is going to be a walking arms depot. Ben, you can't allow yourself to be distracted. Don't move more than a few steps from the entrance. If we have a situation, you may have

163

to crash the gate. You ready?"

"You bet." Webster was a muscular five foot eight inches and his friends in college had considered him a battering ram. He lettered in college on the rugby team and had the scars to prove it. "You say the word, and I'll be right there, Mr. Pointe." Pointe had confidence that Webster could make just about anything happen. Ben Webster was the first person Pointe had hired when he was put in charge of the security team and had never been disappointed. Webster would have two cases. One with the munitions and one with medical supplies that an EMT would covet. Webster had been the EMT at the shootout and had taken care of Pointe.

Pointe continued, "If everything goes to shit, we've got to extract the boss with as little collateral damage as possible. That room will be filled with important people. Rich people. There's bound to be other security people at the meeting."

Then, to Martin, Pointe cautioned, "Chuck if we have a need for medical care, we'll let you know on the way to the airport. What's the flying time to Knoxville from DeKalb-Peachtree?"

Martin replied with confidence, "Twenty minutes. It'll take longer to take off and land than it will to make the trip. The G650 will do mach .85 or a little over 600 mph. Depending on the type medical help you need, I can fly you from here to either Houston or New York in an hour and ten minutes."

"Thanks. We'll rely on Webster to do his thing and keep anyone stable for the flight. Any questions?"

No one spoke up.

"all right, let's rest. Webster and Martin I need to see you two before we turn in. Let's step outside, I need a cigarette."

Gregg, Fanceca and the others on the team went to their rooms. There were drivers for each of the two SUVs and two more footmen. Everyone would be in dark suits, radio equipped, and Kevlar vests. It would be exciting. It could turn dangerous. Would sleep be easy? Gregg wasn't worried, he would often knock down a couple of bourbons and sleep well.

Outside, Pointe was restless. He set the pace and walked

faster than normal. Martin and Webster sensed his uneasiness.

"What's on your mind, Jerry," asked Martin. He had been around the Thibaut organization as long as Pointe and was at ease with everyone on the team.

"We had a team visit Sweeney's apartment."

"He was the mole wasn't he?"

"Yep. How long did you suspect?"

"I had a feeling about him. He tried too hard to fit in. A lot of the new guys do that at first, but he kept pushing," Martin commented.

"Right after the shootout, I had Rosemary send a team in and they found some damning evidence."

"How ironic, that he should be done in by his own people." Martin was incredulous.

"I'm not so sure it was a mistake," replied Pointe. "He had chances earlier and didn't take them. Maybe they wanted him eliminated, too."

"Well, you never know. Here, you need a light?" Martin was quick with the lighter and Pointe was smoking and thinking fast. Martin interrupted his thought process, "How's the shoulder?"

"It's been a long day. Starting to hurt. I'd better take a Vicodin and rest up for tomorrow."

Then Webster joined the conversation, "Are you sure we're clean now? You know, with Sweeney gone. What about Gregg? He's the one here in Atlanta with the least time on board."

"We checked his apartment, too. He's good. Jennifer checked him out. And, he's been working well with Fanceca ever since Cramer got hit."

Webster went in a different and important direction, "Was there any evidence in Sweeney's apartment to give us a clue as to who wants the boss dead?"

"We're working on that. Of course, they're smart and put in plenty of layers of protection. We have a forensic computer geek working on it. All his online communications went through several countries and different types of encryption. The one thing

165

we discovered, is that the connection operates in Europe and has contacts in the States."

"What about another member of the boss's club. You know the meeting he's got tomorrow. Somebody in there gunning for him?"

Pointe looked at Martin and smiled. Then he turned to Webster and replied, "That's one of my concerns. Everyone in that group is ultra-rich. Those types have petty jealousies that remind me of teenaged girls in high school. Stupid shit. That's why we have to be ready to shoot our way in and out of that place. I hope we don't have to."

Webster thought for a moment and asked, "That reminds me. For the pieces I'll be carrying, do you want silencers?"

Chapter Thirty

Brian Farrell and Star Braun were onboard ITTA Corp's private jet en route to the United States. "How long till we hit Atlanta?" Farrell asked Star.

"We've been in the air about an hour, so I guess depending on headwinds, at least a good six hours."

"You brought work to do?"

"Yes, as always," and they laughed.

"OK, what's the agenda?"

"The travel agenda first. The meeting of course in Atlanta tomorrow. We're staying over after the meeting and fly in to Teterboro on Saturday. From there, I'll go into the city to the condo. Are you going to your house in Sparta — or to New York with me?"

"Depends on how tired I am. Do I have to decide tonight?"

"No, of course not."

"Sunday you're off all day and then we hit the ground running in New York on Monday. You'd better rest up Sunday."

"I'm playing golf I think."

"Tomorrow. While you're working the reception, I'll be schmoozing with the bankers and lawyers. Frank is already in Georgia and will meet us there. He will get me an update on the suit and then I'll fill you in later. What are our chances this time?"

"Goddammit, I wish I knew. I'm accustomed to being in control. We know Thibaut will vote against us. I'm not even sure that his one "No" vote can be overcome. Pulling information out of those guys is difficult — hell, it's impossible."

"Regardless of the outcome, I'll be waiting in the condo. If it isn't a celebration, we can still spend the evening with each other. Do you want me to be wearing nothing but water again?"

He didn't react, so she got back to business, "What are we going to do about Griffin Challenger?"

"He's out. Even if I make it onto the council, he's out. I'm tired of his political maneuvering, his games, and his lack of results in his division. I told Warren to start a search for a

167

replacement on Monday."

"Warren told me he'd already started. You know he keeps a file of potential candidates all the time."

"Yes. Is he looking in-house or going outside?"

"He knows you want the best. He has candidates from both," Star assured him.

"This council position is important. You know that it's election year in the States. I want to be in position to have some impact on the 2016 election."

"Is it that important?" Star was sincere. "I mean, to ITTA?"

"I'm surprised you have to ask." She shrugged her shoulders and smiled. She knew he would begin a soliloquy.

"Whether you're talking about the CIA, the Mossad, MI6, whatever, one of their primary missions is to gather, 'otherwise unobtainable information' for their respective governments. Once I'm on the council, that information will be available to me and the management group. It's almost unfathomable how beneficial that information could be to ITTA. Think about it. From entertainment, media, education, and of course, financial — literally every division of my company could make gains in their respective markets."

Then his eyes got big and he rubbed his hands and smiled, "Oooooh damn. Inside information on our competition. All in the name of 'national security.' With the influence of the ambassador of the UK, too. Hmmmm... what we could do for the world would be unlimited."

"How altruistic of you, sir."

The moment the words made it out of her mouth, Farrell seized upon the topic, "'Sir.' Yes, I'm working on knighthood. Warren thinks he can pull that off within the year."

He leaned back with his hands behind his head and looked up lost in a self-indulgent reverie of power, influence, and the respect that would come with that coveted English prefix before his name.

He resumed his speech, "And, yes. It is in fact altruistic.

168

ITTA does wonderful things for people all over the world. We could do much more with me on the council, a lot more, when I'm knighted. I'll be THE knight on the council. Wouldn't it be great to have a seat on the cabinet of the President of the United States?"

"Are you thinking Secretary of Defense?" she asked with a coy smile.

He sat up straight, assumed a dignified posture and spoke in an official sounding tone of voice, "I've always thought that what was good for the country was good for the ITTA Corporation." He looked at her and smiled.

Star began laughing and said, "You sound like Charles Erwin Wilson. But I don't think they'd choose an English knight for the cabinet."

"Maybe they need a knight in shining armor as fucked up as their country is now. But that's another thing. I wouldn't have to be in politics. The council is the grand master puppeteer. It controls the politicians, elected officials and everything — worldwide."

"I've often thought that letting people vote was just smoke and mirrors," she commented.

"It's worked for over 200 years in America. People vote every year for something. Then once every four years for king — er, President."

Star took a breath to speak and said, "You know," when Farrell interrupted.

"Yes, I know. They don't have a monarchy. At least not officially. Did you know that Franklin D. Roosevelt was related to five other Presidents by blood? And that he was related to six others by marriage?"

"I didn't know he had been married that many times." Star laughed.

Farrell kept on, "The American masses are controlled by a ruling class of aristocrats and don't seem to know or care. God, think about all the millions of dollars spent on elections, adverts, and buying votes. Give me that money and I'd do something beneficial for the world with it."

169

"For the world or General Motors?" Star was still smiling.

"At least ITTA doesn't need a bailout. Where's the list?"

They worked their way through her list of subjects and had dinner. No one other than the two of them were on board except the pilot and co-pilot. They served themselves and had a bottle of wine with their meal. When the list was done and the wine gone, the Gulfstream was still about three hours away from Atlanta.

"After next week, the agenda settles down doesn't it?" Farrell asked.

"It's a rather slow week other than the quick day trip to St. Jude's."

"Let's go to Switzerland," he suggested.

"Mmmmm....sounds like fun."

"Lights out now. Tell the captain to wake us up about a half hour before we touch down."

Star Braun silenced the ringer on her cell phone and therefore would not find a new e-mail until after they landed in Atlanta. It would provoke an "Oh shit" reaction. It was from Warren Byrd and read, "In the States. Tennessee State Troopers arrested an armed motorcyclist. When asked for his papers, he began shouting, 'Diplomatic immunity.'"

The Ritz-Carlton Condos are located at the intersection of Peachtree Road NE and Roxboro Road about a mile from the Buckhead Club. The ITTA Corporation owned one of the premier condos with the best view of Atlanta on the property. Farrell had been involved in the project from its beginning and got his choice of locations when occupancy began. The condo was made available to any of the executive team and he and Star had spent many nights there. They had also entertained there often in the last five years.

The company jet touched down at DeKalb-Peachtree on Thursday. A white limo was waiting to deliver the man who would be knight and his fair lady to their mansion in the sky. As they stepped into the limo, Farrell said to Star, "My dreams are becoming real. It's as clear as Stone Mountain on a cloudless day."

170

She smiled.

Farrell continued, "I'm about to make a real impact on the world."

Chapter Thirty-one

Hixon's pickup truck was moving through the mountains towards the Atlanta area at a rapid pace. It had made this trip so often that Hixon joked about setting the cruise control and taking a nap. He was determined to motivate Thibaut into talking on this trip.

"How long you been in this exclusive group?"

"Pass."

"You think it's been beneficial to stay in."

"That I can answer. Yes. It's been beneficial, and I'm not being selfish here, but the council has a number of significant accomplishments for which it can take credit. Meaningful and important works for the global community."

"How altruistic of you, sir."

"Don't ridicule me. Name a significant world event where help was needed and I can show you where we were involved - behind the scenes of course."

Hixon thought a moment, "Haiti. Katrina. The BP oil spill. 9-11. Going back further, Chernobyl." After a pause, Hixon added, "Anywhere money is involved."

"Isn't it obvious?" Thibaut asked.

"Deep Throat was right."

"Of course he was. There are those out there with money who want to help others, think Bill Gates and Warren Buffet. There are those out there who have money, but are reluctant to reveal how and if they use it to help others, think Steve Jobs."

Hixon interjected, "When I think of big money, I think of Rockefeller, Ford, and Carnegie — old money. Because you use some of your money to help the masses, that doesn't mean that you use the rest of it for good causes, too."

"It takes money to make money," replied Thibaut.

"Speaking of making money, can you justify a seven figure income for an executive in a company where sales and profits are driven by some poor working slug who makes fifty cents more than minimum wage?"

"I can do that, but we're off the subject."

172

"How often do y'all meet?"

"As often as necessary."

"So you must have officers. Someone has to call a meeting."

"There's a pickle in Red Square."

"Who killed the Kennedys?"

Thibaut was beginning to tire of the conversation, "Why don't we talk about the FBI for a while?"

"Maybe we should talk about you and me. Who's trying to kill you?"

"I've got people working on that."

"I hope they do better than the ones who were trying to protect you."

"I'm not dead am I?" Thibaut replied.

"You've had some close calls — too close, to suit me. Could it be someone in your secret society?"

"Every member has the financial resources to make it happen. Everyone in our council has similar motivations for being there, Mr. Hixon." Thibaut wanted to be firm, so he was more formal. "We have several things in common. In addition to what the man on the street might consider 'unimaginable wealth,' all of us have strong convictions that our actions benefit the masses.

Of course, we all have agendas. Some of us have agendas that don't match the motivations of everyone in the group. It makes for some interesting debates. At the end of the day, we feel like we're doing what's best for all considered."

"So, y'all decide what's best for the rest of us?"

"Hasn't it always been that way? Were the founding fathers the poor workingmen of the day? How many signers of the Constitution were bank tellers and dockworkers as opposed to the bank owners and ship captains? Think of how many generations that have had the same complaint, that a typical person can't go to Washington and represent the people."

"Wasn't that the original plan?"

"Yes, a man — this was before women's suffrage — would leave his farm or family business and go represent his

173

district at the nation's capital. Then he would return home and live under the laws he helped to pass."

Hixon decided to let a few concerns off his chest, "Now we have career politicians. People with law degrees and degrees in political science who never knew what it was like to have driven a tractor or operated a cash register. And you still haven't convinced me that your group isn't another conspiracy."

Thibaut was beginning to become frustrated with Hixon's stubbornness, "all right. Let's try another example. My father was on the finance committee at his church for years. The chairman was a veteran bureaucrat who saw nothing wrong with deficit spending. Every year he authored and promoted a budget for the church in which spending exceeded even the most optimistic expectations for collections, based on pledges which were not always reliable. Dad and a few of his likeminded friends organized and voted down the budget.

They had the support of the pastor who said, 'We have to be good stewards of God's money.' In the end, they got the man removed from the committee. So, was that a conspiracy? Or was it an example of good judgment by a group of people committed to doing the right thing?"

Hixon was quick to reply, "Now you're trying to convince me that the motivations or intent of the actions of a group define whether or not they're a conspiracy? I suspect that the core group that makes the decision will always feel justified. They'll rationalize their actions every time. And the core group always comes out on top."

Thibaut crossed his arms and looked out the window.

Hixon continued, "Whoever decided to have John F. Kennedy assassinated no doubt did it on purpose and made it clear what they wanted. Nobody said, '"Will no one rid me of this turbulent priest?' in the JFK case."

Thibaut became tense, "God. Do you conspiracy theorists always have to invoke Henry II and Thomas à Becket?"

"Was the murder of the Archbishop of Canterbury a conspiracy? Or was it more like a bunch of zealots hearing what they wanted to hear? While we're on the subject of the church, have you heard about all the internal action in the Vatican? The headlines in the mainstream media have been quick to refer to it as a conspiracy." Hixon wanted to go for the jugular and did so with a non sequitur, "Do you even bother to vote?"

"Pass."

"Well now, you don't need to vote do you?" Hixon wasn't expecting an answer and none came. He went in a different direction, "I guess someone as rich as you has to involve themself in that kind of thing or lose your influence."

"Self-preservation. There are times when I attend the meetings with nothing on my plate. I like to be there and listen. Seek out opportunity in what everyone else is working towards."

Hixon decided to change the subject and returned to his own mission. "Tell me again how we're going to hook up with your guys."

"They'll be there. You told me you saw a couple of my guys in Waynesville."

"Yes. At the bookstore while we were having coffee and you were checking the papers. We didn't make eye contact, but we both saw each other. They watched you like hawks while you were looking for a paper."

"That's good. They'll be there in force. Didn't you tell me Pointe got hit?"

"Sure looked like it to me. May have taken a shot in the back."

"Somewhere on the way into the meeting they'll make their presence known. They'll wait for me to react. I'd prefer to stay separated. Maybe if they're working the crowd, too, we can learn more."

"You think somebody is going to make an attempt on your life at the meeting?"

"If at all, either before, after or during the reception. No one would dream of doing anything inside the meeting."

"Here we are." The pickup was slowing down and Hixon turned into a strip shopping center in Roswell, GA.

Hixon said to his client, "Sit tight a minute." Then he got out first and checked around the parking lot, making a bit of a

175

show of his efforts to provide security. He walked over and opened the door for Thibaut and they walked into the Goodwill store.

As they entered, Thibaut turned to his body guard and asked, "Goodwill?"

The big man laughed and said, "It's a front. But years from now, you'll be able to look back, laugh, and tell your ultra-rich friends, that you wore a suit from Goodwill to one of y'all's big meetings."

Hixon then led the way through a curtain in the back near the fitting rooms. They continued down a narrow hall and into an office filled with books. The sign on the door read, "Area 51." The walls were lined with bookcases and each was overflowing. Most of the volumes were hardbound editions. Few of the books appeared new or unread. The room reeked of cigarette smoke and the singular inhabitant was holding a flaming Zippo about to light another.

Robert Dillon was an inch or two short of six feet tall. In spite of his age, his hair was thick, and true to his hippie reputation, long. It was parted in the middle and with his big nose and bushy mustache, he reminded Thibaut of Frank Zappa. His face had too many wrinkles for a sixty-three year old. Maybe he had spent too much time in the sun. Maybe he had dealt with too much stress. In contrast to his physical appearance, his hazel eyes sparkled and betrayed his enthusiasm. Thibaut thought to himself, *I thought hippies were supposed to be laid back. Maybe I'll have the opportunity to ask him about his stress. Maybe I would if he didn't speak in lyrics.*

"Bobby, this is my friend, Jay. Jay Thibaut, Robert Dillon." Hixon introduced the two.

Dillon smiled, they shook hands and Dillon said, "Now all the authorities, they just stand around and boast." His voice sounded like a piece of tin as it was rubbed by an old file. It was a deep raspy sound, reminiscent of a terminal COPD patient. His prolonged coughing made you think he was choking and provoked the unpleasant image of a thick expectorant dotted with bits of lung tissue.

176

Hixon interrupted, "Bobby, we're in a bit of a tight timeframe. Jay here wants a navy blue three piece suit. I'm thinking a dark gray for myself — single breasted. I'm too big to look good in a double breasted coat.

"The geometry of innocent flesh on the bone." With that, Dillon turned and opened an antique armoire, produced a tape measure and went to work measuring Thibaut. "Once upon a time, you dressed so fine."

Hixon requested, "Can you finish 'em by mid-afternoon?"

"You say you never compromise." Dillon replied.

To Dillon's surprise, Hixon replied in a melodic, "Do you want to — make a deal?"

"There's no reason to get excited — the thief he kindly spoke."

As Hixon stepped towards the door, he said, "When you ain't got nothing, you got nothing to lose."

Chapter Thirty-two

After a visit to yet another Waffle House, Hixon and Thibaut returned to Dillon's Area 51 in back of the Goodwill store at the agreed upon time. When they arrived at the book- and smoke-filled office, their host met them at the door, extinguished his half-smoked cigarette and led them down the hall to another door, labeled, "Whatever fits."

It was a clean, well-lit dressing room with chairs and long handled shoehorns hanging off their backs. On racks next to each chair hung two pair of suits. One pair was gray and one pair blue, as requested.

Dillon turned to his customers and with one hand presented the fruits of his labor with a flourish that would have made Bert Parks happy. He announced, "You must pick one or the other, though neither of them are to be what they claim."

Hixon said with pride to Thibaut, "How about that. Two suits for each of us. Let's try 'em on."

Hixon put on his shoulder and ankle harnesses and ended up with the coat of one suit and the pants from the other. Of course the material matched. Dillon had planned ahead. Thibaut's suits both fit to perfection and he took both. While the two men were getting dressed, Dillon had slipped out of the room and returned with shirts, ties, and black wing-tipped shoes for each.

Julian Thibaut thanked Dillon and asked, "What do I owe you for such fine work in such a timely fashion?"

"The man in the coonskin cap wants eleven dollar bills — and you only got ten."

Thibaut paid many times the request in cash and included a generous tip. As they were leaving, Dillon smiled his approval and said, "We'll meet again someday, on the avenue...tangled up in blue."

Thibaut shook his head and turned to Hixon. "Now it's off to the hotel?"

"Almost. We have one stop to make first. I arranged for a taxi to pick us up about half way from here into Atlanta. It'll look better if we don't pull up at the hotel in a pickup truck, don't you

178

think?"

Thibaut nodded in agreement.

"Which hotel is it you've got rooms?"

Thibaut said with authority, "I always stay at the Intercontinental."

"Well, we're staying at the Holiday Inn Express in Marietta. It's right on the way and I don't want to lose the element of surprise by being seen at one of your old haunts."

"That makes sense. I'm beginning to like the way you think, Mr. Hixon. What time is it?" Thibaut hadn't worn a watch nor paid much attention to the time since the shootout.

"It's after five." Then, looking at his watch, Hixon reported with precision, "It's five fifty p.m. You hungry?"

"No. Maybe we can eat later?"

"Fine, but I want to go out to eat before we shave and I want us to be in our 'mountain clothes' in case we still need cover. Have you ever eaten at a Cracker Barrel?"

Thibaut speculated, "I wonder if Elvis ever enjoyed eating out at a restaurant like the common everyday man?"

"There were numerous reports that The King often helped out total strangers. He stopped muggings and bought Cadillacs for strangers and friends. There's even rumors that he was an undercover agent for the DEA."

"No. I've never eaten there. Is it as good as Pasquales? I enjoyed our dinner that night."

"Totally different atmosphere and cuisine. Cracker Barrel is louder, more casual and has great home-cooked food. If you like supper there tonight, we may go back for breakfast. When do we need to head over to the Buckhead Club?"

"We should arrive there a little after six. Cocktails start at six and I want to work the crowd. It will be interesting to see the looks on the faces of those who think I've disappeared."

Their cab was entering the exit ramp from the interstate and Hixon perked up, looking this way and that, surveying the landscape as though a sniper could be lurking behind any available cover. Hixon handled the transaction at the front desk and let Thibaut carry his own luggage. He thought to himself, "I

179

bet Mr. Jay hasn't done this much of his own work in a while."

They found their room and began to settle in. Hixon kicked his boots off, grabbed the remote for the television, piled up several pillows, and began to surf the channels.

Thibaut unpacked, laid out his gear and hung up his new suits. In the bathroom, he put his hands on the counter and leaned in close to the mirror. He had not shaved in several days and was surprised at how much gray was beginning to show up in his beard. He stepped back from the counter and crossed his arms. Then he moved his right hand up to his face, fingers on the left cheek, and thumb on the right. He puckered his lips and then turned to look at himself in profile. He tried to imagine what he would look like with a full beard, or maybe a mustache.

How long had it been since he had availed himself of such an opportunity for self-examination? Most of his introspection had avoided a corresponding look at himself. His staff and assistants had offered suggestions. Standing there alone, looking in the mirror, he began to think about his life and his future. Questions surfaced. *How many of Hixon's words had hit home? Did he really need to stop and smell the roses?*

He remembered reading about a recent social experiment arranged by *The Washington Post*. They put a concert violinist in a train station playing some of the best music ever written on an instrument worth millions. This performer had sold out a venue at $100 a seat. In forty-five minutes at the train station, only a handful of commuters had stopped to listen. A long loud snore from the bedroom interrupted his reverie.

Thibaut waited until the snoring became rhythmic. He walked in a casual manner into the room and noticed that Hixon's hand had relaxed. The remote had fallen onto the floor. The History channel was showing a documentary about Hitler and the Jews told from the point of view of an American soldier that had served with Patton. *How could that have put Hixon to sleep?*

Thibaut smiled and left the room without a sound. Once outside, he checked to see if he could hear the snoring. If the sounds of the world at war didn't arouse his roommate, sure the click of the door latch wouldn't — and it didn't.

In the lobby, he approached the front desk person, "Is there an 'old man's' bar nearby?"

The young Asian man responded with a blank expression.

Frustrated, Thibaut turned away and saw an older African-American man dressed in hotel apparel who was smiling. He had overheard the request. Their eyes met. Neither man had to adjust his gaze. The Black man spoke first, "I know where you want to go. I got off work a few minutes ago. Every evening I stop by a small neighborhood bar on my way home. Would you like to join me?"

Thibaut noticed the name badge and said, "Well, Ted, please call me Jay."

"Ted ain't my real name. I forgot my name tag this morning and I borrowed this one from a fellow worker — Theodore." A huge warm smile preceded his introduction, "My name is Abe. Another President." Then a big laugh. Abe led the way to the employee parking area. As they walked, Thibaut observed his host. Abe Region had not had an easy life. His gait was not smooth and the wrinkles on his face and hands made him appear older than he probably was. They got into an early seventies model four door sedan that must have been twenty-five feet long — a Lincoln Continental Town car.

Thibaut complimented Abe, "You've done a remarkable job taking care of this thing. It's beautiful."

And it was. "I didn't come by it new, and it was in sad shape when I got it. The lady that sold it to me had worked for it. She got a good deal. She kept house and watched the kids for a man in Atlanta. He was overpaying her anyway, but she agreed to fifty dollars a week less if he threw in the car." He laughed a high pitched repeating sound that would have sounded like crying if you couldn't see him. "She did work for them several more years, and they were both happy with the car deal."

"How did you 'come by' it? If you don't mind me asking," Thibaut inquired.

"Oh I don't mind. I drove by her house about six months after she passed. I was on my way somewhere else and cut through her neighborhood. This car was sittin' on four cinder

181

blocks out in the front yard."

"What did you have to pay for it?"

"One of the neighbors offered me $50 to haul it off." and they laughed.

Abe turned the whale of a car right onto Franklin Road SE and continued until they reached the Social Security Office. He pointed it out and said, "We like to come to the Louisville Tavern 'cause it's close to our favorite office building," and another laugh.

An F-22 Raptor screamed in, almost hitting the treetops, and Thibaut reacted. Abe comforted him, "Don't be alarmed, Dobbins Air Force Base is right across the street," he pointed straight ahead and they saw the jet touch down. Thibaut was impressed with the relative ease with which Abe parked his long car. The sign out front was shaped like an inverted letter "T" with the word Louisville printed vertically in what years ago would have been considered white. The aged letters were on a background of red metal that had been rusted through and now appeared orange. The word "Tavern" was on the horizontal axis across the bottom. Empty brackets that years before had served as the mountings for tubes of neon light dotted the edges of the lettering. Once inside, Thibaut was won over on the spot with the charm of the "old man's'" bar. It was as he had hoped it would be. The barroom was long and narrow. It was dominated by the old fashioned wooden bar. There was enough room to walk to the other end of the room without disturbing anyone that might have been sitting on the barstools. At the far end were booths along the wall and two tables that would seat four, if anyone wanted to sit there. Competition for table seating was nonexistent.

Abe introduced Jay to three of his friends in the booth closest to the bar and three more seated at the corner of the bar. They welcomed him like an old friend returning from a long absence. The old men clamored to buy his first drink. Everyone was eager to hear his story and ask him a thousand questions. He was thrilled with the reception, surprised at their acceptance and charmed with their interest and enthusiastic desire to learn more about him. Thanks to their efforts, an immediate rapport was established.

Back at the Holiday Inn Express, Thibaut entered the room making no effort to be quiet. It wasn't necessary. Hixon was reaching for the door when Thibaut opened it.

"Where the hell you been? I was on my way to go looking for you."

"I took a long walk around the property. Wanted some exercise and to check to see if there was a pool and workout room."

"It's almost nine. If we're going to eat, we better hoof it on over to the Cracker Barrel."

"Let's go. I'm starving," Thibaut agreed.

Hixon smiled and asked, "When was the last time you had meatloaf?"

Chapter Thirty-three

The following morning, the reluctant partners ate at the breakfast buffet inside the Holiday Inn after sleeping late. Thibaut continued his interactions with the everyday people, much to the surprise and delight of Hixon. On each trip through the lobby Thibaut had found someone with whom to chat. He had eyed the computer terminal set up for customers to use free and summoned up the self-control to avoid logging into his e-mail account. Later, on their way to lunch, Hixon surprised him. "I've got a disposable cell phone. Do you want to alert your folks with a text? In a few hours we'll be arriving at the meeting."

Thibaut typed in "See you at the mtg" and hit "Send." He returned the cell phone to Hixon who stepped on it and then baptized it in the fountain of the court yard. He tossed it in the garbage can on the way into the Cracker Barrel. They lingered over lunch and Thibaut confessed his recent whereabouts.

Hixon was pleased to see the subject of his current occupation had returned safely. It was clear that he had had a good experience.

"John, you should have been there. These old men were great. They ranged in age from about sixty-five to up in their eighties. The bartender was an older man, too. He goes by the name, 'Louie' — for the tavern. Not sure if it's his real name or not. They obviously had known each other for years and years."

"You enjoyed yourself, did you?"

"Yes. It was interesting, thought-provoking, and eye opening. You'll love their first names."

"Yeah? Why?" asked Hixon. He wanted to know more.

"Former presidents — Abraham, George, Thomas, Woodrow, Franklin, Ulysses, and Ronald. These guys were excited and animated. Raising their fists, gesturing. Sometimes they laughed when they said something, sometimes they seemed to be dead serious. It was hard to tell when they were teasing. One man claimed he had voted for Obama five times. Another said he had voted for Lyndon LaRouche five times to counter the five Obama votes."

"I thought LaRouche was dead," Hixon commented.

"No, but he hasn't run for office since 2004. A couple of the men seemed to be well versed about politics and world affairs. I asked them how they came by such information and you know what they said?"

"What?"

"One said he watches CNN and the other said he watches FOX. And then the whole group burst into laughter. Anyway, back to LaRouche. Did you know that he had served time?"

"No. What for? Election scams?"

"You're going to love this: conspiracy."

"You gotta be kidding? Did he kill Kennedy?" Hixon was smiling now.

"No, of course not. He was convicted for conspiracy to commit mail fraud — and then there were some tax violations, too."

"What else did y'all discuss?"

"One of the other Black men, not Abe, had read a recent article in *Ebony* magazine and was disappointed with Samuel L. Jackson who had revealed that he voted for Obama just because he was Black. One of the old Black men said, 'That's just as racist as the other way around.' They covered a lot of ground from the price of gold to the price of oil, oil spills, income taxes and the increasing number of people who depend on the government as their sole source of income. Did you know that Macao is still a hot spot in the world gold market? It's long been known for black market gold bullion."

"Did y'all talk about abortion and gun control?"

"Ran out of time. We closed the place down," and Thibaut laughed. "I haven't been in a bar at closing time since my college days and never one that closed at 8:00 p.m."

Hixon asked, "To use some of the new-wave, politically-correct, management jargon, 'What did you take away from your visit with the old men's club?'"

Thibaut was energized, "I'm telling you. You'd love those guys. Claim they advise local law enforcement and politicians."

Then he answered the question, "Maybe a new regard for

185

people who need other people to look out for their best interests. These guys don't trust corporate executives any more than they trust politicians and bureaucrats. They spoke highly of Warren Buffet and Bill Gates because of their philanthropic endeavors — but they still don't trust them. They got all over Trump. Then they got close to discussing my group. One of them said something that hit home with me."

"And that was...."

"The discussion was centered around how few people control everything and that more input was needed. One of them, I think it may have been Ron, said, 'You can double a small number, but you still have a small number.'"

As they finished lunch, Thibaut surprised Hixon with another bit of news. "These guys told me about an old-fashioned barber shop not too far from here. Let's go over there for a shave and haircut after we shower. My treat."

After their visit to Nick's Barber Shop, they got back to their room and finished dressing. Thibaut wasn't surprised at Hixon's gear, not after their experiences over the last few days.

Hixon noticed Thibaut admiring the pistol that would go into his shoulder holster. "It's a 1911 .45 semi-automatic. I've got several extra magazines in case of problems. It has real knockdown power. Designed for use in the tropics when foot soldiers had to stop onrushing natives who were hopped up on drugs."

Hixon called for the taxi and a half hour later, they were on their way.

Thibaut sounded wistful, "We're about to be a whole world away from your cabin in the mountains."

"I'm no stranger to your world. I haven't been in it in a while and I don't miss it at all. By the way, do you know the name of this expressway?"

"Saw the sign when the limo entered the ramp, 'Larry P. McDonald Memorial Highway.' Wasn't he a U.S. Congressman from Georgia?"

"Yes he was. Know anything else about him?"

"Wasn't he killed in a plane crash back in the eighties?"

186

"Yep. Korean Air Lines Flight 007. Easy number to remember. Guess what his middle initial stands for."

"Don't tell me."

"Yes sir. Patton. They were cousins. Something else not too many people know about — at least not today. Back in the eighties it was well known that McDonald was the president of the John Birch Society."

"Wasn't Birch a missionary?"

"Bravo." Hixon was elated. "You hit the jackpot. John Birch was an American military intelligence officer and a Baptist missionary in World War II. Some people consider him the first casualty of the Cold War."

"And to what do we attribute your knowledge of Mr. Birch?"

"No doubt, you've heard of the organization that bears his name — or you're playing me. I worked a case or two when I was in the Bureau that, let's say, caused me to become educated by and about the John Birch Society."

"Ah, conspiracy central," Thibaut baited him.

"I'm confident they know more about your exclusive group than Mr. Jimmy or me. They won't be out picketing in front of the Buckhead Club, but it looks like the folks from 'Occupy Wall Street' are here with their Atlanta delegation."

The taxi had turned the corner and approached the entrance. Hixon was right. There were about a hundred protesters all around the entrance and main parking area. A local news group was there with a van sporting a telescoping antenna for live broadcasts.

Thibaut still wanted an understated arrival so he directed the driver to a less crowded portico. As they drove past the main entrance, Thibaut noticed Gerald Pointe out of the corner of his eye. He was standing with Webster who was holding a typical looking brief case, although Thibaut knew what was inside. They had been waiting in the common area before the metal detector and internal security.

Thibaut turned to Hixon and said, "My guys are here. Let's see how effective that badge is in helping you pass

187

security."

Part Seven

The lady behind the desk at Planned Parenthood of Hackensack, New Jersey looked up and gave her patient a weary smile. It was the morning after Thanksgiving, 1976.

"Is that your real name?"

"It's that obvious?" asked Claudia.

"Honey, I've heard 'em all. When are you due?"

"Early December."

"Take this folder and go wait in room 3 down the hall. It's on the right."

Twenty minutes later, Dr. Chiang entered the room and sat in a chair next to Claudia. "You look great. I was hoping to see you once a month, not once a trimester," she scolded with a smile.

"I've been busy. The baby was a surprise and working around previous commitments that involved travel has been difficult. But it all worked out. I feel great, too."

"I'll be back in a moment and we'll take a look at you. After the exam, I've got some news for you. The details are in my notes and I'll bring them with me."

Dr. Chiang was in a cheerful, upbeat mood, "My husband and kids will be in Taiwan most of December, so the timing is great. In fact, they're leaving the Monday after Thanksgiving. Are you still confident with your decision?"

"Yes. I've debated all the pros and cons and I want to do what is best for the child. What kind of arrangements have you been able to work out?"

"Private adoptions are best kept secret — from everyone. My experience has been good and there is one attorney in particular that does private adoptions with great attention to detail. I also want to make sure that it's crystal clear that you won't see the child. Just a few minutes after delivery, a nurse will take the infant to another room where a medical team will do an assessment and then clean. Many times, newborns need some degree of medical care. If the infant is sent to the nursery, you'll be moved as soon as possible to the women's health unit in another part of the facility. As soon as the infant can travel, the

189

attorney and yet another nurse will leave the hospital with the child and meet a couple who will serve as foster parents for a few days. When he delivers the baby to the adoptive parents, all legal records will appear as if that woman was the birth mother. He requires that there be no way you can ever trace the transaction and when the child is grown, it will not know it was adopted. This is severe and final. You must understand that in advance."

"I do. In fact, I have no plans to stay in Hackensack and doubt I'll ever live in New Jersey."

"OK, then. You call me if you begin labor, here's my direct line and my pager. If not, we'll go ahead with plans to induce on December 7th."

Three hours later, Claudia walked into the lobby of the Chelsea Hotel in Manhattan and was surprised to see her old friend waiting in the lobby. "Mr. Debert." For some unknown reason buried deep in her subconscious, she had always referred to him formally as "Mr."

"Claudia. You kept me waiting." he said with a jovial laugh.

"I've had a great day and a wonderful afternoon. Slow paced and deliberate. I finished my appointment in Jersey just before lunch. Went to my favorite deli, 'Gerdes,' for a salad. The checkup was fine and we're set to go for Pearl Harbor Day."

"Wonderful. Would you like to join me for a drink in the bar?"

"Sure. I'll have tea though."

"I know. Didn't expect you'd have alcohol."

They walked together across the lobby and into the bar. Claudia spoke first, "I love this place. It feels like home — and it also reminds me of New Orleans, in particular, the wrought-iron works on the balconies and staircases."

"Have you stayed here often?" Debert asked.

"Yes. Every time I come to New York. I don't visit New York City as often as I'd like, but I hope to in the future. My trips to the Northeast don't always bring me here. I went up to Cape Cod back in the summer of '74 before I got started in the master's program at LSU. It was great. Do you like lobster?"

190

"Any way you serve 'em." Debert was in a concerned mood. *"You say you got things finalized today in New Jersey?"*

"You know I've made a career decision too, don't you?"
"Yes. You told me last time." He frowned. *"It's disturbing. We'll talk about it again, I'm sure."*

"Please, not now, OK?" she demanded with a question.

"What about the father?" He expressed genuine concern.

"We haven't talked about him, have we?" Claudia felt the need to do so. *Perhaps discussing this would help confirm her own feelings. Did she need more reassurance?*

"It could be one of two men and one of them is dead. The other wouldn't make a good father under the best of circumstances and it would be my word against his. Blood tests aren't conclusive and, well, I couldn't count on him for money or any other support anyway. Abortion isn't my choice."

"Why not? I thought you were pro-choice."

"You've known me a long time, Debert. I believe a woman should be free to choose. So I made a choice. You know how I was raised and by whom. You know my religious background, it's nonexistent. What I know about man and God and law I've learned in classes and from books I've read. How many people do you know that can say that 100% of their visits to churches have been as tourists? Huh? How many?" she was pressing him.

"None."

"I've visited courtrooms to study body language, seating arrangements and behavior more than I've been into churches. And speaking of body language, when I can feel something inside me kicking and moving around on its own, without my conscious influence, well, for me, that's life and I'm not going to end it. You never know, it could turn out to be the president one day — or better yet, a great world leader." She smiled. Debert already knew her opinion of politicians.

"Doesn't it bother you that you won't be able to share in this child's accomplishments?"

"One of my classmates was a woman who had returned to school after the kids were gone. But it wasn't because they had

191

grown and gotten married and left home to start their own lives. In this case, her husband had left her and convinced the kids that the divorce was her fault. They sided with him and when I met her in school, they hadn't spoken to her in over two years."

"You seem to have a response for every point I bring up for discussion."

"My choice was not easy. The decision is final and arrives after much thought. You know those logic puzzles that are so popular?"

Debert nodded.

"Well, I've applied a similar thought process to many different situations that I could face as a single mother. Look around. It's 1976 for Pete's sake. This isn't post-World War II America still recovering from worldwide trauma. There are a few single mothers around — more than thirty years ago, but still not many. And in lots of communities, they're still ostracized for staying single."

"You never struck me as one who would bow to 'what others think.'"

"I'm not. I have always been career-minded and like to think of myself as one who cares enough for those I love to do what's best for them."

"What about the price you pay in terms of your mental health with this decision?"

"Aha. No problem at all there. I'm looney tunes already." She got a smile from Debert.

"My biggest risk is trusting that the right family has been chosen to be my child's parents. That's a huge leap of faith for me. It's like being a tightrope walker without a net — and I'm doing cartwheels on the high wire."

Debert pressed on, "It's clear that your career choice had a major influence in your putting the baby up for adoption."

"Picture this. First grade teacher has each child stand up and talk about their family. My kid stands up and says, "I don't have a daddy but my mom makes lots of money killing people."

"You're right. That wouldn't sound good," replied Debert, playing along.

192

"Besides, it's too late now anyway."

"What do you mean?" Debert became concerned.

"I've already killed someone. Two, in fact."

There was a long silence. Debert was stunned and speechless.

Chapter Thirty-four

Randy Randle had a guest. The knock on the door was not answered. A thorough look around the hallway confirmed that the middle aged man was alone. He used his own key and entered the room. Once inside the room a speedy transformation occurred. Within minutes, the visitor had become a punk girl.

Claudia Barry had become, "The Shooter."

The long auburn wig and the colored contacts would complete her disguise. Those details would take a minute or two after the mission was completed. The shooter then began to assemble her rifle and chamber one of Hixon's "heart attack" rounds.

The M-110 SASS (semi-automatic sniper system) was developed in 2005 for U.S. Army snipers and has been used in Afghanistan and Iraq since 2008. The rifle with sound suppressor attached was almost four feet long. The shooter liked the M-110 and handled it with ease. Including a twenty round magazine, it still weighed in at just over fifteen pounds. The custom suppressor from Hixon's shop had tested well. There was minimal loss of muzzle velocity and superb sound reduction. With the ambient city noise and a vacant room on either side, the shot should go unnoticed.

She took a position near the open balcony door and began to survey the target area through the scope. The positioning of the sun should be favorable. The subject would work the crowd and then walk right into the cross hairs. The setting sun would make him a silhouette to those in the room with him and obstruct their view of the shooter's position. Perfect.

Below, the first limos were beginning to arrive and deliver their privileged cargo. Farrell was fashionably late.

And here is the famous Farrell, said the shooter.

His personal assistant, Star Braun, and his attorney, Frank Gravelle, were with him.

The usual entourage.

The shooter was ready.

The time was near.

He'll be working the reception soon.

The butt of the rifle came to rest with comfort. It was secure and rock steady against her shoulder. Through the scope, she searched the room for her target.

There you are, Farrell, you magnificent bastard.

She took a deep breath. It was for these moments that she had practiced holding her breath for longer and longer periods of time. The contents of all the sealed compartments would have been obliterated from her consciousness hours before. She, the rifle, the bullet and the target became one — in the moment.

The target moved as it always did and required minimal adjustment by the shooter.

You've got your audience, now, stand still and start talking.

She held her breath and nothing moved other than the index finger on her right hand. For the shooter, there was nothing romantic about this job. As she had written in her journal a few days before, "You romanticize death if you haven't been there and seen it happen."

Chapter Thirty-five

Inside the Buckhorn Club, Hixon had reverted into a persona that he once thought he had left for good. In spite of his size, he was dapper in his new Dillon suit and he moved around the crowded room with ease. "Jack Daniels and Coke," he told the bartender. And after this one, I want the same glass with straight Coke. I'm on duty."

The bartender noticed Hixon placing a twenty dollar bill into the tip jar, made eye contact, and winked. Hixon took his drink, turned around and looked for Thibaut. He had to stay close to his man.

The banquet room hosting the reception dominated the southeastern end of the building and had glass walls on both the south and east sides. The evening sun was setting to the east of the neighboring Intercontinental Hotel's tower and dominated the view from the windows facing south. It was so bright as to be uncomfortable now, but would afford a beautiful sunset in an hour or so.

Hixon had to work hard. Thibaut was a pro when it came to working a crowd. Shaking hands, introducing Hixon, asking about common interests. Hixon grew tired of the fake smiles and endless handshaking. He was concerned that if he did need to use his gun, he would have carpal tunnel pain from all the hand shaking. When they tried to take a break, someone would approach the mismatched pair. What an odd couple they made. Hixon towered over his client and grew concerned that his cover wouldn't last throughout the evening.

In the rest room, Thibaut confirmed, "Look John, you're doing fine. If I tell someone you're my assistant, then you are. In this group, no one questions me. Now, listen, have you noticed anything unusual?"

"Your guys are near and Pointe moves like he got hurt pretty bad at the shootout."

"I noticed that, too."

"What's next?" Thibaut was ready for the "closed door meeting" to begin. He wanted a break from the reception. Maybe he could visit with Pointe before joining the meeting.

"There's still a few more people I need to schmooze and some more for you to meet. There's a knockout Scandinavian woman out there whom everyone wants to know in the biblical sense. I'll introduce you to her."

Back in the banquet room, they could sense that the reception was about to break up. The typical small groups were beginning to scatter and people were queuing up at the bar for a last drink before the members repaired to the private meeting room.

There was one exception. A group of about a dozen people were gathered around a speaker who had their attention. Applause had interrupted his impromptu speech more than once. The entire group was near the windows facing south and were all in silhouette against the setting sun. Thibaut was about to take Hixon over to join them when a couple intersected their path.

Thibaut acted pleased to see them and shook their hands. He turned to Hixon and said with almost genuine sincerity, "Let me present Miss Star Braun of the ITTA Corporation and their corporate attorney, Frank Gravelle."

Hixon stepped forward and shook their hands. His great palm and long fingers dwarfed theirs and his firm grip was almost painful. Thibaut asked, "Where's Brian?"

Star motioned over towards the silhouetted group and laughed, "He's holding court over there in the spotlight of the sun."

Thibaut held his hand over his eyebrows to shield the sun and said, "It's so hard to see with the sun, but it looks like he's grabbing his chest."

At that moment, Farrell was indeed grabbing his chest and collapsing to the floor. Hixon did not have to think twice to know what was happening and dropped his glass on the floor with an extra push, so that the sound of it breaking would attract attention. With the instinct of a mother bear moving to protect her cubs, Hixon stepped between Thibaut and the windows to shield the sun so that his client could see better. He had often and habitually provided the same service to many companions.

Hixon's broad frame was an effective shield to the sun.

Miss Braun and Mr. Gravelle rushed to check on their company's president. Hixon felt what he would later describe as "being hit by a baseball bat on my right shoulder blade."

A simple gesture of common courtesy earned him his fee for everything Thibaut had hired him to do.

He took a bullet for his client.

The sniper's round had penetrated Dillon's custom made suit and the first layer of Kevlar as if nothing were there. A similar round would slip right through a steel plate like a hot knife through butter. The hollow point mushroomed upon entering Hixon's flesh and shattered its way through his right shoulder blade. There was little left to stop it until the completely opened round reached the Kevlar on his chest.

The impact would have knocked a smaller, less balanced man off his feet. Even with his bulk and stability, Hixon was staggered. He reached out and put a massive hand on Thibaut's shoulder and with that support, never lost his footing. From nowhere, Pointe and Gregg arrived and offered quick support as they rushed both Thibaut and Hixon out of the reception hall.

At the first sign of trouble, Pointe had alerted Webster who had produced the Uzi from his case and pushed his way past the guards. The metal detector went off as Webster passed through.

Hotel security had called 911 and the stage was set for pandemonium.

Pointe, Gregg, and Webster shepherded their boss and Hixon out the front door and found their limo waiting but blocked in as it was third in line. When Pointe had sounded the alarm barely two minutes before, one of Thibaut's SUVs had jumped the curb and bullied its way near the entrance. The five men jumped in and the vehicle sped away. Pointe was on his secure cell phone to Chuck Martin, "Fire. We'll be there in half an hour, maybe sooner."

"I'll be ready for takeoff. When you're close, call me. I'll ask the tower for emergency clearance for your vehicle. Meet me at the end of the strip. As soon as you board, we fly."

"Thanks, Chuck. If the tower gives you any shit, call Rosemary. No wait. I'll call her myself. We've got contacts. She'll take care of it."

"Status?"

"One hit, stable but bleeding. Boss is fine."

Webster had changed roles and assumed his duties as an EMT. He turned to Hixon and asked, "What's your blood type?"

Chapter Thirty-six

Now, after a costume change, Claudia was in character as the punk princess. She stepped through the door of Randy's room into the hallway. Her gear was stowed neatly inside a cello case. There was a man several steps ahead of her in the hall and the sound of the door closing caught his attention. He glanced over his shoulder and Claudia was stunned.

Oh my god. she exclaimed to herself, *It's Debert.* Her first thought was, *Stay in character. I've fooled Jacques before, I can fool Debert, too. I'm the last person he would expect to see here.*

Debert, ever the gentleman turned, smiled and turned on the charm, "We're going the same direction. May I accompany you to the elevator?" She smiled and noticed that he wasn't looking at her face.

"Thank you, but I'm taking the stairs," she tried her best to alter her voice. She hoped he wouldn't recognize it.

Then they each noticed what the other was carrying. She had her cello case and he had a longish case that looked familiar to her. She spoke first, "Cello. I'm on my way to an audition."

Debert's response sounded cold, honest and was shocking, "I'm a professional assassin and this is my sniper's rifle."

She was at a loss for a reply. Then he rescued her with a broad smile and a hearty laugh. They approached the door to the stairs and he held it open for her. She stepped through, bounded up several flights, taking two steps at a time and then stopped, listening. There was not a sound other than her panting and she felt comfortable that she was alone. Even with her aerobic prowess, a dash up several flights of stairs at her age required some recovery. She had waited for this moment and let out a tremendous sigh of relief, followed by a victorious laugh. It was a well-earned display of earnest enthusiasm. Her unique release of that god within. At this moment she personified the feeling of which many could only dream.

Now it was time to change roles and make her exit.

The bellman waited as the little hump-backed lady with

blue hair stopped by the front desk to deliver a personal "thank you" to the manager for a wonderful stay. "We appreciate your business, Miss DeVille. We hope when your travel plans bring you back to Atlanta, we will see you again."

She smiled and turned towards the bellman who was tending the luggage cart with all her bags and shopping booty. He helped her to the curb and a waiting taxi.

"Where to ma'am?" the driver asked.

"Dunwoody Plaza shopping center — and make it snappy mister."

A few days before, she had arranged for a car to be waiting for her there from Enterprise Rent-a-Car. She liked the fact that they would pick you up or meet you. At the shopping center, she went into a public restroom and Miss DeVille ceased to exist.

A young man in white shirt and black tie carried several suitcases and some shopping bags down the sidewalk to a UPS Store. By the time the car arrived from Enterprise, several packages were on their way to Tuckaseegee, North Carolina, to Mr. Jimmy's General Store.

Two hours later, Robert Dillon went to the door when he heard a knock. It wasn't heaven's door. Was it Hixon's friend? Could it be "Sweet Melinda?" In the darkness of his living room, he racked the slide on his pump shot gun and pulled the thin curtain back from the small diamond shaped window in his front door. Hixon's pickup truck was parked out front. The all denim-clad person at his door didn't appear to be female. Claudia spoke first with an amended version of the lyric, "I speak good English — but I won't invite you up into my room."

Dillon's eyes lit up. He relaxed and leaned the shotgun against a nearby easy chair. When the door opened, Claudia stepped in and asked, "Have you heard anything from John?" "He looked so fine at first, but left looking just like a ghost."

She wasn't sure what that meant. "Is he ok? What have you heard?"

Her eccentric host shrugged his shoulders and shook his head. Without speaking, he offered her a cigarette. She waved it off and said, "No thanks, but if you've got a bottle of vodka, I'll help you drink it."

Dillon's reply was so typical, it made her smile, "Kick your shoes off, do not fear. Bring that bottle over here."

It was hard to resist replying in kind, "And I've waited all day long, for tonight when I'll be staying here with you."

She sent the text that seemed redundant but necessary for confirmation, "Target neutralized with extreme prejudice." She lay down on Dillon's old but comfortable couch. It would be a long sleepless night waiting for word from Hixon that would not arrive.

Chapter Thirty-seven

It was almost 8:00 p.m.

Louie the bartender at the Louisville Tavern was about to make his last call for the evening. The regulars were sitting around one of the tables playing dominoes as they often did. The television over the back of the bar was on *Headline News* and as usual, ignored by the men preoccupied with other, more important concerns.

Unnoticed by Abe and his friends, CNN financial reporter, Bill Tucker, was on the screen reading from the teleprompter, "Spokesperson for the UK ambassador to the United Nations, Maggie Chamberlain, announced moments ago that London based businessman Brian Farrell died today of a massive heart attack while attending a meeting in Atlanta at the prestigious Buckhead Club. Farrell was CEO and Chairman of the Board of the international ITTA Corporation. There has been no official statement from the company, but Chamberlain said memorial services would be held in London next week. [PAUSE] In other business news today, Julian Thibaut announced that his firm, Double Entendre Investments, will begin studying ways to help the typical middleclass 'man-on-the-street' have a more active role in government."

Louie announced the last call and one of Abe's older friends, Ronnie, shouted out back at him, "Fuck you Louie. We ain't leaving till we finish this game." Everyone laughed.

Chapter Thirty-eight

Chuck Martin clicked on the mike after receiving clearance to land and informed his passengers, "Touchdown in Knoxville in ten." As predicted earlier, their flight time had been nineteen minutes.

"It's been a little over an hour since you got hit, how you feeling now?" Webster asked. He and the other EMT had been working on Hixon's wound since they got into the van. It had taken almost 45 minutes in Friday evening rush hour to drive from the club to DeKalb airport. The shooter had used a bullet meant to kill. It had mushroomed and disintegrated. What little remained was embedded in the front side of the Kevlar vest Hixon had been wearing.

"It hurts like hell. I thought that shot you gave me would help more than it did. What was it?"

"Demerol and Vistaril." Webster replied. "We also started an IV line so when we hit Knoxville, it'll be easier to get more meds into you. From the angles, it looks like the bullet went right through your shoulder blade, maybe hit a rib or two and exited an inch above your right nipple. I'm concerned about blood loss and internal injuries. Your right lung could be a problem."

"Can I pass out now and sleep this off?"

"We'd rather keep you awake for now. So far, we've been able to keep you from going into shock. There's a van waiting in Knoxville to transport you to our emergency care center. They can operate if necessary, and it looks like you'll need it."

"Shit."

Thibaut stopped by on the way to his seat. He offered his right hand and Hixon reached up with his left. It was an awkward but meaningful handshake. Their eyes met, "Thank you. You saved my life, I'm certain," confirmed Thibaut.

John looked up and managed a smile, "That's what you paid me for. But now, I may have to charge extra. I'll send you a bill."

"Fine. The check's in the mail."

Throughout the flight, Thibaut and Pointe had been

204

catching up on each of their adventures since the shootout at Deal's Gap. Pointe relayed the message that their attacker on the Dragon's Tail had been apprehended, arrested, and asked for diplomatic immunity. Thibaut's reaction was calm.

"That confirms what I suspected all along."

Now they were seated next to each other fastening their seat belts as Martin began his final approach.

Thibaut asked Pointe, "Where did you find that guy, Hixon?"

"Friend of a friend of a friend. You know. I always work my network. He was recommended by someone that has never let me down."

"And they were correct. Sharp guy. A bit eccentric, as are his friends, but he's someone with whom we want to maintain contact."

"A life or death experience bonds a friendship that may not always be good for the long term."

"That thought certainly crossed my mind. Hixon and I had several lengthy conversations that went a lot deeper than typical 'get acquainted' stuff. I met some of his friends and he's met some of mine. The man has integrity."

"Did he ever take Taekwondo?"

"Why do you ask that?"

"From what you've said about Hixon in the last hour or so, it sounds like he fits their mold. The tenets of Taekwondo are: honesty, integrity, perseverance, self-control, indomitable spirit."

"Did you know he was in the FBI?"

"Yes," Pointe answered.

Thibaut smiled and said nothing.

Chapter Thirty-nine

Claudia's Delta flight to Grand Cayman Island arrived at Owen Roberts International Airport at four fifty-nine p.m. With the anticipated announcement, she turned off her Kindle and stowed it away in her carry-on bag. The night before she had downloaded a dozen novels. Lots of reading to do. She had plenty of time to rent a car, drive up to Seven Mile Beach and find her rental unit. She preferred to rent a small one bedroom cottage and spend lots of time on the beach. All those years of avoiding the sun and protecting her skin were behind her now. She wanted a nice golden tan. The property manager met her and conducted a brief tour.

"The reservations said you would be here a few weeks. Is that still accurate?"

"Yes. I'm looking forward to a nice tan, light reading and then do some painting."

"Water color or acrylic?"

"For years, I've done mostly acrylic. I may try some watercolor now."

"You're in the right place for some inspiring and dazzling sunsets."

"I know. I'm thinking about driving out to the east end and visiting the reserves."

The manager left and she changed into a two-piece swim suit, covered herself with tanning lotion and walked down to the beach. The blue waves came in and hit the shore in a relentless rhythm. Looking out towards the horizon, they appeared as layers of blue ridges and reminded her of the mountain view from Hixon's cabin. She missed the mountains.

She had changed her viewpoint from the crest of a mountain to the edge of a shore. She had not changed her plans. It was disappointing to have not heard from Hixon after the mission in Atlanta. One night at Dillon's house was all she could stand anyway. The idea of visiting Mr. Jimmy had crossed her mind but she would wait — it was too soon.

The surprise meeting with Debert in the hotel had been

unnerving. *Was he a sniper? Why was he there? Will he show up here in the Caribbean?* There were several things that needed sorting out. She wanted to take a nice long, solitary stroll this evening. It would be nice to watch the sunset and then walk back to the cottage after dark.

As she walked along the shoreline, she remembered a concept she had heard about many years before. She thought to herself, *"They said that 'self-actualization' is when what you do for a living is a complete and total expression of who or what you are as a person. I'm sure many people yearn for that experience. Was I self-actualized? Was killing thirty-eight people the real me?"*

She shuddered at the thought. She turned cold even though the temperature was still in the high eighties after sundown. The moon was only a sliver of light. Was it time for her to start a new life?

She spoke out loud as she would if Debert had been near, "If your work is your life, how do you retire from living? I've always lived alone, no time for anyone or anything else. Maybe I'll look into adopting a pet. Do brick masons quit laying bricks totally after they retire? Will I be able to lock forty years into a sealed compartment?"

Later that night she would write in her journal, "I'm living the result of my life's work. I am alone. I have to start a new life and forget the past. Do other retirees enjoy wonderful memories of their careers? I cannot speak of mine. Any word I utter must be screened. All my life I enjoyed being a 'self-styled recluse.' Now I'm stuck in a world devoid of anyone. Maybe I could write fiction. Novelists are never lonely. They spend hours and hours in the company of imaginary people they create and control. But I could publish an authentic diary and the world would think it fiction."

Chapter Forty

After her vacation in the Caymans, she went to Geneva for six months. It was the coldest six months of her life. The flight into Newark had been rough. She had never gotten sick before and this time she had emptied her stomach before the jumbo jet reached calm air space. The view of the Manhattan skyline from Hoboken was always a treat — and a reason for a visit to the Northeast. Maybe a visit to Cape Cod in the summer. *Yes*, she thought. *That would be nice.*

The assigner had not been pleased to hear the news of her intention to retire. After much debate, they agreed on a year sabbatical. *How absurd*, she thought. *After another year goes by, I'll be in my mid-sixties. Too old for this job. And yet, my age would be a great cover. Who would ever expect?*

The last message from the assigner had ended with, "Stay in practice."

The next morning, Claudia set up her easel in Frank Sinatra Park on the Hudson River in Hoboken. Today's medium would be watercolor. The blurred lines and edges melting across each other by the extra water on the paper before the paint was applied had begun to appeal to her. It was a subconscious message. Open the sealed off compartments. Life is less stressful when the lines are blurred.

Claudia came here for the view facing east. Tomorrow she had reservations for lunch at the Irish Pub in Manhattan where she had first met Mr. Debert. Maybe he would be there again. Maybe he would find her alone at a table as he had before, so many years ago. He had not visited since they had shared breakfast in Sandestin. Where did he come from? She had seen him last in the hotel in Atlanta when she was dressed as a punk girl. Had he known it was her? Did he realize how much she missed him? Was he real — or a creation of her imagination? She needed him to help answer the questions on some of those compartments that she had sealed years before. She needed him to exist. Maybe he could help her reopen the compartment that contained her lover, John Hixon. The man she missed even more than Debert.

The following morning she decided to drive into Manhattan. Driving in the city wasn't her favorite task. She often took a hired car. Focusing on traffic would be yet another form of escape. Thanks to the rain, even more concentration would be required. The traffic light was changing and there was plenty of time to stop. No sense risking it on a rain slicked street. Too bad, this was one of the longest lights in Manhattan. The shooter relaxed and watched the rain collect on the windshield as the wiper blades paused for a few seconds between cycles. First it was images, then text. It was like e-mails appearing on the screen of her computer but now they were appearing on the windshield right before her eyes. No time to read them as the wipers cleared them away with each wave. Always changing, more messages and no time to read nor savor them.

"Did my targets realize their own frailty, their vulnerability, their mortality? Were they able to adjust the length of time the blades of fate hesitate between each event?"

The light changed, the pace of the rain quickened and without a thought, her hand came up, her finger touched the lever, and the wipers went from intermittent to regular speed — with no pauses.

The End

Watch for the sequel:
A Year Without Killing by Claudia Barry.

Preview a story of political intrigue, featuring John Hixon: *The President's Club* by FCEtier.

The Presidents Club

Chapter One

Louie the bartender had a sawed-off shotgun under the bar. His hand was on it as he spoke to the man at the end of the bar. "I've heard enough of your foul mouth and I'm sick of your dirty jokes. It's time for you to pay and go."

The patron with the ugly laugh stood and slowly looked around the bar. He looked Louie in the eye, threw a ten-dollar bill on the bar, and said, "Don't go home alone." The tough guy with dirty teeth, greasy hair and filthy fingernails waddled out of the Louisville Tavern dragging his feet on the tile floor.

When he returned to his duties, Louie noticed Simon Franklin's glass was almost empty. "Want another draft, Simon?"

"I'll just finish this one and head on home."

Louie remembered what Simon had said earlier and asked, "You seen Dean Rusk or Colin Powell lately?"

"No. Rusk died years ago and Powell's staying under the radar. Maybe on speaking tours."

"How long were you at the State Department?" asked the bartender.

"Too damned long," sighed Simon Franklin as he stood to leave. He slipped his hand into his pocket and Louie took a few quick steps and waved off his customer's intention to pay. "Simon, you've only had one. Tonight, it's on the house."

"Thanks, Louie. I appreciate it. I'm gonna walk on down to the bus stop, y'all have a good evening."

"Watch your step," Louie called out to him, "it's darker than usual." Simon was almost through the swinging doors into the foyer on his way home.

Louie quickly moved back to the far end of the bar

211

to answer a question that had been shouted out by one of his regular customers, Woodrow Risk. "I don't know much about him Woody. Tonight was the fourth night in a row he's been in, had one beer, and left."

Risk returned to a game of dominoes with three friends and Louie resumed polishing shot glasses and beer mugs.

Out on the street, Simon Franklin paused for a moment to let his seventy-four-year-old eyes adjust to the street light — or what there was of it. Louie had been correct. The light on the utility pole was out, making the street around him much darker than usual. He could hardly see the edge of the sidewalk and the gutter. Two more steps and he would see better. Store signs, traffic lights and a few cars passing helped light his way to the next corner. A right turn and a two block walk to the bus stop and then he would be home free.

A voice called out down a nearby alley. Simon stopped. His heart rate quickened. He could not understand what had been said. The sound of boots hitting the pavement faded as the runner got further away. It was darker than he had anticipated. He breathed a sigh of relief as he consciously worked on calming his body's response.

His respite was short-lived as the sound of footsteps approaching from behind got his attention. A drunken, ugly laugh broke the silence on his path ahead. The darkness seemed to tighten around him as he stood alone near the opening of an alley.

"Who's there?" he called out. His voice broke like that of an adolescent reaching puberty.

The ugly laugh became a low growl and demanded, "Get on your knees, old man."

Simon felt fingers grasp the collars of both his jacket and shirt and push him forward. An unsure step forward left him standing but unstable. The fist was keeping its victim from falling.

212

"I said get on your knees," the voice growled again in a much more menacing tone.

"I can't," Simon managed to say between tearful sobs, "I got bad arthritis." He was crying and trembled like a dead leaf trying to cling to a branch in a gusting wind.

A second attacker struck. A short quick swing, almost like a bunt or a check-swing with a baseball bat, across the back of both knees crumpled the victim as the fist released its grasp.

Barely conscious, Simon listened to what he feared might be the last words he would ever hear, "Tell your presidential friends they're next. One at a time." The dark night drew tighter still. Simon Franklin lost consciousness.

"Is he still alive?"

The fist that moments before held the victim with such callous disregard now tenderly touched the neck and felt a pulse. "Yeah. If he don't stroke out on us or go into cardiac arrest, he'll live to deliver our message."

"Grab his foot, I'll get the other one, and let's drag him down close to the bus stop on Franklin Road."

"See anybody?"

"Naw. The coast is clear."

A tall slim man whose eyes missed no detail waited while an EMS crew pushed their way through the open double doors to the Kenestone Hospital emergency department. He adjusted his tie and took several deliberate, confident strides towards the check-in desk.

He exhibited the self-assured demeanor of a hospital administrator.

Few people in the busy emergency room noticed him.

The ones that did thought he was a lawyer.

He was neither.

Most were self-absorbed in their own dilemmas.

213

Stabbings. Auto accidents. Gunshot victims. Hand to hand combat in a bar room.

The regular crowd had shuffled in.

A twenty-something black male was in line ahead of the sharp dressed man. When asked, the patient told the receptionist, "I've been shot."

"Again?" It was obvious she was annoyed. "Where?"

He pointed to a small cut in the hairline just above his forehead. He turned and she could see where the slug had skimmed between his skull and outer layer of skin and lodged in the back of his head.

She directed him to an empty chair and said, "Sit over there for a few minutes and we'll bring you a Band-Aid." Then she looked at the man in the business suit with hope in her eyes.

"I'm detective Falconer with the Marietta Police Department. You called me about a mugging victim?"

"Thank you for coming down so quickly, detective," said the front desk lady. She opened the door and took him to the triage nurse. Nurse Reilly led him to one of the curtained-off treatment areas and said, "Our patient may not live through the night and the director thought you might want to talk to him."

Falconer asked for confirmation, "He was awake when the ambulance brought him in?"

"Yes, barely. We got him stabilized and then he mumbled a few words and passed out."

"What exactly was it he said before he lost consciousness again?"

"What he said, is why we called you." Nurse Reilly flipped a page on the chart and read, "Tell the President he's next."

20359501R00126

Made in the USA
Charleston, SC
08 July 2013